DOUBLE BARREL

DOUBLE BARREL

THE SILENCER SERIES BOOK 13

MIKE RYAN

WWW.MIKERYANBOOKS.COM

1

Recker looked around the office, feeling as uncomfortable as he could remember. It was pretty much like he expected it to be. There was a desk, a couple of chairs, a couch, and a bookshelf with a lot of titles that looked hard to pronounce. He promised Mia that he would come to see if it helped with his sleeping issues, but he didn't think it would do much good. Going to a psychologist's office might have worked for some people, and was probably a good idea, but just wasn't his cup of tea. Opening up to some stranger about life wasn't in his DNA. But for Mia's sake, he agreed to give it a shot.

Dr. Louise Penner was highly thought of, and was recommended to Mia by co-workers in the hospital. She looked over the sheet that Recker filled out in the waiting room, though his answers weren't very in depth. And some of the questions he skipped. Even the name threw her for a loop. John Smith. She had a feeling this was going to be one of those kinds of patients that really tested her skills. Some patients freely opened up and she could barely get a word in. This was not going to be one of those. She sat down across from Recker.

"So, Mr... Smith. Tell me about yourself."

Recker looked stunned, as if he weren't ready for the question. In truth, there wasn't much to say about him. Or much that he would say. "Well, I'm, uh... I'm... here."

Penner grinned. "Very good. I can see that. So is Smith your real name? Because some people have a habit of coming in here with fake identities, thinking they can't reveal who they really are or something."

"Sure."

"I promise you that anything you say in here, it just stays between us. No one else."

"OK. Good."

"So tell me about yourself."

Recker coughed. "Well... I have a girlfriend."

"Good. What else?"

"That's pretty much it."

Penner couldn't help but laugh. "OK, well that's a good start. What do you do for a living?"

"Well, I, uh... really can't say."

"All right, is it because you're embarrassed about what you do or you would rather do something else? Are you out of work?"

"No."

"You're a... man of few words."

"Usually."

"So tell me about your girlfriend."

"She's a nurse."

"Good. And?"

"That's it."

"Oh. So let's get back to your work. Is that why you're here?"

"Maybe."

"So can you explain what you do?"

"Not really."

Penner rubbed her hands together, realizing this would be a real challenge. "OK. So what's stopping you from talking about it? Is it that you're uncomfortable? Don't want to? Can't?"

"Uh... can't."

"OK. So are you in a secret line of work?"

"You might say that."

"Do you work for the government? Police?"

"Somewhere around there."

"OK. So your job swears you to secrecy?"

"You might say that."

"OK, well, that's a start. Is that why you're here today?"

"Could be."

"What exactly are you having problems with?"

"I have... sleeping issues."

"OK. What kind?"

"I usually wake up in the middle of the night after having a bad dream."

"And what are the dreams about? Are they the same ones or different?"

"Different sometimes. Sometimes they're the same, but sometimes they have variations to them."

"OK. And is there a general theme to them, or do they vary wildly?"

"Usually they involve someone close to me getting killed."

"Oh. OK. So what do you think that means?"

Recker grinned. "If I knew that I wouldn't be here."

"How long have you been having these dreams?"

"I don't know. At least a year probably."

"Is it every night? Do you have them with the same occurrence or regularity as before?"

"At first it was not very often. Once every few weeks, a couple months, something like that."

"And now?"

"It's probably four or five nights a week. I'm usually more surprised when I don't have one than when I do."

"I'm gonna take a wild guess and say that with your secret job that it can sometimes be stressful."

"Usually."

"And dangerous?"

"Sometimes."

"That probably has a lot to do with it."

"That's what I figured."

"In your line of work, have you had people close to you who have passed away in that work?"

Recker's eyes hit the floor, immediately thinking of Carrie. "Yes."

"Do you think that the dreams might possibly reflect your apprehension about possibly losing more people you care about?"

"Maybe."

"Are you ever the victim in these dreams or is it just people around you?"

"Sometimes me. Sometimes others."

"OK, so let's talk about your mindset."

Recker didn't really want to talk about his mindset. Or anything else, really. Though he knew it wasn't how it worked, all he really wanted was an answer on how to make the dreams go away, or put his mind at ease. He didn't really want to get into his feelings or explain them. For the rest of the session, which lasted about forty-five minutes, Recker did his best not to reveal too much of himself, or delve into too many topics he didn't want to get into. It was tough trying to keep a secret life a secret. Or revealing who he really was.

"OK," Penner said. "Well, our time is up for today, but this was a good first session. I think we accomplished a lot here."

"We did?"

"I think so. Let's set up another session for next week and we can dig into things further. What do you think?"

Recker waved his hand in the air. "Yeah, maybe."

Penner could see his hesitancy, but wanted to make sure he didn't blow her off after only one session. She had plenty of them. Some patients decided one session was all they needed, and some decided the setting just wasn't right for them. She thought Recker was a deeply conflicted individual who would really benefit from multiple sessions. He just had to make them.

"I think we can really get to the bottom of your issues and take a significant step forward with them with a few more sessions. So make sure you make them."

"Well, with my job, I have a tendency to not make plans too far in advance."

"That's OK. If you have an afternoon free or the next day or whatever, just call and see if I'm available. If I am, I can fit you in on short notice."

"OK."

Recker walked out of the office and saw Mia sitting there, a smile on her face.

"So, how'd it go?"

Recker shrugged. "I dunno. She wants to meet again."

"Well that's good."

They walked out of the office building and strolled along the sidewalk, their arms locked together. It was a busy day, with a lot of people walking around them.

"What do you think about lunch?" Mia asked.

6

"I think I could be persuaded to dine with a pretty woman."

"So what do you think? Are you going to see Dr. Penner again?"

"I don't know. I don't know if it'll really help."

"But it can't hurt, can it? I mean, even if it does wind up not helping, it's certainly not going to make it worse. And the best-case scenario is that it does."

"I hate it when you talk sense."

"I know it's not comfortable for you and you're out of your element there, but I really think you should keep at it. At least for a few more sessions."

Recker nodded and smiled. "I probably will."

Mia reached up and kissed him as they continued walking to the restaurant. They were only a few minutes away from it, standing along a street corner, waiting for the crosswalk sign to change to green. As it did, Recker and Mia started walking along the white lines on the road. Once they got near the other side, Recker's eyes happened to glance at a car driving nearby. There was just something about the car that captured his attention for some reason. Maybe the fact that it was starting to speed up while everyone else was slowing down. As the car turned the corner, he noticed the window beginning to slide down. This was one of the times when he felt a problem was coming before it actually existed.

Recker slowed down, letting Mia get in front of him, so he could shield her in case there was an issue.

As the car got near them, Recker turned his head back to look at it, seeing a gun emerge from the window. He immediately pushed Mia to the ground, diving on top of her as several bullets ripped through the air. The car quickly sped off after it missed its chance at The Silencer. Luckily, none of the bullets hit anyone else either, as all of them either hit the ground or the wall that was behind them.

"Everyone OK?" Recker asked. There were several other people on the ground near them.

After getting confirmation that everyone was, Recker turned to Mia, helping her up. As she brushed herself off, she looked at him.

"You knew. You pushed me down before the bullets fired."

"It was just a feeling. You know I've always had that sixth sense when trouble is near. I just had one of those feelings."

"So who were they shooting at? And why?"

Considering he was who he was, Recker was pretty confident he was the target. It would have been too big of a coincidence for him to be at a spot where someone else was the target, or that it was just a random occurrence. No, he was as sure as could be that it was him.

"What did you get yourself into now?" Mia asked.

Recker looked at the direction the car travelled off into, long gone by now. "I don't know. But I aim to find out."

2

As Recker and Mia finished their lunch, she looked at him and shook her head, laughing at him.

"What?" Recker looked down at his shirt. "I make a mess or something?"

"It's just you. You just get shot at, and here you are, eating, talking, like nothing ever happened. Like it doesn't even bother you."

Recker shrugged. "Because it doesn't."

"How can you be so calm?"

"Well, for one, I don't know for a fact it was me. We just suspect it. And two, I've been shot at before. It's not exactly a new feeling. And three, they're obviously gone, so there's nothing else to worry about now."

"Unless there's someone else waiting outside here."

"There's not."

"How do you know?"

Recker shrugged again. "I just sense it."

"What are you doing, using your Force powers?" Recker smiled. "So why would someone be after you?"

Recker shook his head, unable to come up with anything. "I don't know. We're not really in the middle of anything major. Just the regular stuff."

"What's more alarming is they knew where you were. How would they know that?"

"Lucky guess?"

Mia glared at him. "Mike, be serious. I mean, it would be extremely coincidental if they just happened to be driving along and saw you and decided to take a shot. I mean, what are the chances?"

Recker grinned. "Not real high."

"Exactly. So that means someone had to tell them where you were. Who else would know?"

"Nobody. Nobody knew I was coming here except for you."

"Well I sure didn't tell anyone."

"That only leaves one other explanation then."

"What's that?"

"We were followed."

The look on Mia's face said it all. "Somebody knows where we live?"

"Have to. That's the only other explanation unless we go with the happened to see us while driving theory."

"That's scary. What are we gonna do? I don't know if I can stay there by myself when you're out, knowing that someone tried to kill you and also knows where we live."

"We might have to make other arrangements."

"But that's our home."

Recker tried to comfort her. "Our home is wherever we're together. That place, it's just four walls. Well, it's actually more than four, but you get the point. It's just a place that we live. Wherever we go, as long as we're together, that's our home."

Recker pulled out his phone and called Jones. He let him know everything that happened and asked him to start going through camera footage to see if they could figure out who the shooter was. Once he was done, Mia didn't even let Recker get the phone back in his pocket before peppering him with questions.

"What'd David say?" Mia asked.

"He's gonna start looking into it."

"That's all."

"That's all we can do right now." Recker then put money on the table to pay for the meal. "We have to go, though."

"Why?"

"Got a job coming up. Gotta get back to the office."

"With this looming over our heads?"

"David's looking into it. He'll find something. Until he does, there's still people out there that need help."

"And what am I supposed to do? I can't go back to the apartment all alone. If they know where we live, how do we know they won't be there waiting for us?"

"We don't. I'm not taking you back there right now."

"Where am I supposed to go?"

"Guess you're going to the office."

Recker and Mia left the restaurant and went back to their car. They drove back to the office, where Jones and Haley were already waiting for them. Mia gave each of them a hug upon seeing them, after not seeing either of them in over a week.

"Any cuts or bruises?" Haley asked.

"No, I'm fine, thank you," Mia answered.

"Find anything out yet?" Recker asked.

"Not yet, but it's still early," Jones replied. "I'm confident we'll come up with something. You were downtown and there's cameras all over the place, so I'm sure something will turn up soon."

"Let's just hope it's not a dead end, or a stolen car or something like that."

"Well, we'll just go where the clues lead us. We will figure it out. We always do."

"Yeah. So you said we got a job coming up?"

"Sure do." Jones looked down at the papers on his desk and found the one he was looking for, handing it to his partner.

"What's this?"

"What's it look like?"

"Car theft?"

"That's what it is."

"That's a new one."

"Car theft is new?"

"New for us."

"Yes, well, those two gentlemen on your sheet there are planning on taking a few cars in that neighborhood in approximately one hour. So you two need to get there and prevent that from happening."

"Sure about the time?" Recker asked.

"Positive. One texted the other to confirm the time."

"What are they doing with the cars?"

"They are planning on taking them to chop shops and getting money from the parts."

"Neither has a big record."

"But they both have records, albeit small, and they will go through with this if they're not stopped. So you two need to do that."

"Nothing that shows they're violent?" Haley asked.

"No history of it," Jones answered.

"Doesn't mean there won't be a first time," Recker said.

"It also means it's not likely. I'm sure you'll be able to handle them through non-violent means."

"Should we hand them milk and cookies and tuck them into their warm snuggly beds when we're done?"

Haley couldn't help but laugh, though Jones kept a straight face. Jones was going to respond but really had no words to say and just shook his head instead. He then pointed at the paper and kind of waved at it, and at the door.

"Just go, prevent some bad things from happening," Jones said.

Recker went up to Mia and gave her a kiss. "We'll figure out the rest when I get back."

She nodded, then sat down next to Jones as he checked some of the area camera footage. Recker and Haley left, taking separate cars to head down to the area of these supposed car-jackers. They got to the area, a run-down residential area on the west side of Philly in plenty of time. They each cruised around the streets, looking for their suspects. Jones printed out mug shots for each of them so they'd have a clear picture of who they were looking for. For twenty minutes they drove around, neither of them finding either of their targets. Recker and Haley kept in communication while they drove.

"You think maybe they got spooked?" Haley asked.

Recker looked at the time. "I dunno. We did get here early. It's right at that time now. We'll give it a few more minutes."

They continued driving for another ten minutes before Haley finally noticed the first one. The car was parked along the street and the man, who was barely above twenty years old, was trying to get in through the driver side door. Haley abruptly stopped his car as he pulled just behind the other car. He jumped out and put his hands on the back of the man's shirt, twisting him around. The man swung with his right hand, hitting Haley across the face, just above his eye. Haley lost his grip of him and the man took off running. Haley dabbed at his face, seeing a trickle of blood on his fingers, though it wasn't too bad. It wasn't something that would need stitches.

Haley looked at the direction the guy took off in, but knew it was unlikely he was going to find him again. He shook his head as if he were trying to clear the cobwebs. He did get hit pretty hard and by something that felt like metal. He felt his head again and sighed, feeling like he blew it. He went back to his car and hopped in, calling Recker immediately.

"Hey, just found one."

"Good, I'm still looking for the other," Recker said.

"You might be looking for a while."

"Why's that?"

"The dude slipped away from me. Probably hightailed it to meet his friend and split the area."

"Yeah, if they met back up after running into you, then they probably think it's too hot and will wait for another time." Haley sighed loudly into the phone, and Recker could tell he was frustrated. "No big deal. They're small-time car thieves, not murderers. They'll get caught soon enough."

"Yeah, I know, it's just... I was sloppy. Saw him jiggling with a car, went in there with my guard down and he clocked me one. I should know better."

"Happens to all of us at some time. You all right?"

"Yeah. He just hit me with something. Might have been metal."

"Let's get back to the office so Mia can check you out."

"I should be fine. It's just a small cut, nothing big. I'll be fine. I wanna cruise around and look for these guys again, just in case they didn't get the hint and are still in the area."

"All right."

They went up and down the streets for another half an hour, not running into anyone that looked like their suspects. Recker was right. The duo got scared off.

"Head back to the office now?" Haley asked, now convinced the pair was gone for good.

Recker had other ideas, though. "Not just yet."

"Where else you wanna check?"

"Not here. I've got a hunch about something. Follow me back to my apartment."

They drove back to Recker's apartment; him having a feeling that someone may have been there watching. It was the only way someone would have known where he was to take a shot at him. With him and Haley patrolling around the parking lot, they hoped to find someone sitting in a car that didn't look like they belonged. Once they got there, they each drove around, not seeing anyone in a parked car. They also got out and walked around the complex, looking for the same thing. They still came up empty, though. Recker and Haley met back up by their cars.

"I don't see anything unusual," Haley said.

"Me neither."

"Maybe it was just one of those fluke things. Wrong place at the wrong time. It's rare, but it does happen."

"Yeah. But it doesn't feel like it would happen to me."

"What about an off-duty police officer? Your picture has been distributed to them. Maybe one of them saw you, one that's not in your fan club, and decided to take things into his own hands."

Recker lifted his cheekbones, not buying it. "Eh, I don't think so. If that was the case, I'd think they would just call for backup. They'd probably get a bigger name and a bigger career boost by being the one that arrested me and brought me in instead of being the one that killed me."

"Yeah, probably right."

"Well, while we're here, might as well go check the place out."

They went up to Recker's apartment, but it didn't take long for them to see that something was wrong. As soon as they got to the door, they could see that it was ajar.

"I assume you didn't leave it like that," Haley said.

"No."

Both men stepped to the side of the door and removed their guns. Recker motioned to his partner that he'd go in first and look to the right and for Haley to go in the opposite direction. Recker pushed the door open wide, the two of them standing there for a few seconds to see if anyone jumped out at them. Since nobody did, and they didn't hear anything either, they went inside, both men already in shooting position. They went through each room, though they didn't find anyone. Whoever was in there was gone. But not before they took the place apart. There was a mess everywhere. Clothes in the bedroom were on the floor and the bed. Items from the bathroom closet were scattered about. Cushions and magazines were on the floor of the living room, with tables turned on their sides, furniture moved about. Even the kitchen was a mess. Cups, plates, silverware, all were out of their homes and thrown about the counters and floor. Recker went over and closed the door as they put their guns away.

"Somebody was looking for something," Haley said. "Sure made a mess of things."

"Yeah, but what? And why?"

"And how did they know this was you?"

"I think it's pretty evident now that I was followed earlier."

"Who would know to do that? And who would have it in for you who's got the means to do it?"

As Recker looked around at the mess on the floor, his mind started racing with possibilities. Two of which he hated to think about, as it would mean that someone had turned on him. The other wouldn't have been pleasant either, but it would have made sense.

"As far as I can tell, it could only be three people that could do this."

"Who?" Haley asked.

"One would be the people we used to work for."

"I thought you were on good terms now?"

"As far as I know I am. But who knows? Maybe something's changed. Maybe there's a new boss who's got a stick up his ass and wants to do things."

"Maybe call Lawson and see."

Recker nodded. "Yeah. The other possibility is maybe The Scorpions are regrouping. They somehow got a hold of where I live and are looking for payback."

"Now that would make sense. I don't see how they would know to look here, but I could see it being them. What about the third one?"

The last one on Recker's mind was equally disturbing, but it would also fit. "Vincent."

"Ahh, I don't know about that."

"I don't know about it either. I don't see why he would. But we both know things change in this business. Maybe I stepped across the line on some of his deals or something. Maybe he's planning something big and wants me out of the way."

"He's had plenty of chances before. Plus, it doesn't seem like his style. I mean, what would he be doing messing around in here? Plus a random shot on the street? Seems sloppy for him. If he wanted you dead, there's plenty of easier ways he could get it done. He could just call you for a meeting and then do it there."

"Yeah, I agree. So if we think that's the most unlikely, I'd say that narrows it down to the other two."

"Well, the CIA does know where you are. As for the Scorpions, if it's them, they'd have had to follow you from somewhere. Maybe a meeting with Vincent that they were watching."

"Maybe. Or maybe they followed Mia."

"Whoever it is, we need to figure it out soon," Haley said. "Because one thing's for sure. If they tried once, they'll try again."

3

Recker and Haley drove back to the office, not giving Jones or Mia a heads-up about the apartment being broken into, or about the car-jackers eluding their grasps. When they burst into the office, Jones and Mia immediately spun their chairs around to welcome the two back. Their eyes were instantly drawn to the new cut that Haley was sporting.

"Well, looks like you two had quite the time of it," Jones said.

Mia got up from her chair and walked over to Haley, dabbing at his eye. "C'mon, sit down." She grabbed his arm and led him over to a chair so she could clean him up better.

"It's really nothing," Haley said.

"Doesn't look like you'll need stitches."

As she cleaned up his wounds, Jones inquired

about the events that led up to that. "Is everyone else still living?"

"What?" Recker asked, hardly even giving the carjackers another thought. They were basically an afterthought to him at that point. He was more concerned about his other situation. "Oh, them. Uh, no, they got away."

"They did?"

Jones was surprised as it wasn't normal that they didn't complete an assignment. What was even odder was how unmoved Recker seemed to be about it. In those rare cases when they didn't complete the task, he was always upset about letting someone get away. But the expression he had on his face now indicated he just didn't give a rip.

"What exactly happened out there?"

"Listen, those guys don't really matter," Recker replied. "They'll get caught soon enough. Right now, we got a bigger problem."

"Oh?"

"After those guys slipped away from us, Chris and I went back to my apartment." Hearing that drew a sharp look from Mia, who turned her head. "Someone broke in and dumped it upside down."

"Someone broke into your apartment?"

"Someone broke into our place?" Mia asked. She was now finished with Haley's face. "Why? What were they looking for? What did they want?"

Recker shrugged. "No idea. I mean, I don't have any trade secrets there or anything."

"You know, I was thinking," Haley said. "Maybe they broke in to plant a listening device or something."

"You usually do that without anyone knowing you were there, though," Recker replied. "You usually don't advertise it."

"Maybe that's it though. Reverse psychology. With the place a mess, that's probably the last thing you would think of to look for because you assume someone wouldn't be that sloppy."

"Someone knows where we live," Mia said.

"What are you going to do?" Jones asked.

"We gotta move," Recker answered. "We can't stay there. It's not safe."

Jones got up and walked over to the window and looked out. "Are you sure someone wasn't watching and followed you here?"

"I'm sure."

"How would this have happened?"

Recker then went over his three theories of who he suspected it might have been.

"It's probably me," Mia said.

"What?" Recker said.

"They probably followed me. I probably got sloppy or wasn't paying attention or probably didn't do what I was supposed to."

"It might not have been you, we don't know that."

"If that is the case, though, that would also mean

they know where she works," Jones said. "That brings up an interesting dilemma in its own right."

Recker sat down and rubbed his head. "My head hurts just thinking about this stuff."

"To me, that brings it down to either the CIA or Vincent. Scorpions don't know about her."

"There was that little incident in the hospital," Haley said.

"But the ones responsible for that are dead."

"That's true."

"I have a hard time believing that it's Vincent," Jones said.

"That's what I said," Recker replied.

"Why?" Mia asked. "He is a criminal, and he did kidnap us."

"He did not kidnap us," Jones replied. "He was the one who got us out of that situation if you recall."

"Yeah, well, maybe. But I still don't see why you guys are always so trusting of him."

"Because he's never given us reason not to," Recker said. "Is he a criminal? Yes. Has he ever gone against us? No. Has he ever turned his back on us or not been there if we really needed him? No."

"There was that thing with the police officers being shot that you thought he was involved with if you remember."

"I'm not saying he's a saint. I just think if he was going to turn on us, there would be better ways for him to do it."

"Well then if we don't think it's him either, that brings us down to one," Jones said. "But what would be the point of that?"

"I don't know. How's your scans coming along?"

"Still working on it. I don't think it should be too much longer."

"Why would the CIA be after you again?" Mia asked, the concern evident in her voice. "After helping them not that long ago."

"We don't know that it's them," Recker said.

"Perhaps you should call Ms. Lawson and find out," Jones said.

"Already put a call into her on the way back here."

Almost as if someone was listening, Recker's phone rang. It was his CIA contact.

"Hey, saw you called," Lawson said. "What's up?"

"Just wanted to... well, I'll just cut straight to the point."

"Don't you always?"

"Someone took a shot at me on a random street corner earlier. Then someone broke into my apartment."

"OK? You don't exactly shy away from that kind of stuff, as I recall."

"I just want to see, uh..."

"Oh, I see where this is going. You wanna know if it was us."

"Well, yeah."

"I thought we were on good terms now."

"I thought so too."

"As far as I know you're a distant memory. I haven't heard anything about you since you came back from London."

"Maybe someone's looking at old cases that had asterisks?"

"There's no asterisk by your name anymore, you know that."

"I thought I knew that. I just wanna make sure."

"All right, hold on. I'm just getting to my desk now." Recker could hear her starting to type away on her computer. "I'm getting into the system now to check your file."

"So?"

"So I can see if anybody else has logged in and if they did, what they looked at, or what they were looking for."

"Oh. I didn't know all that was logged."

"Are you kidding? Are you sure you worked here?"

Recker laughed. "Us field agents aren't always versed in what goes on back in the office."

"So I notice." Recker listened to her typing away. "Find anything?"

"Going through the logs now." Lawson cleared her throat. "I don't see anything suspicious. The last time anyone looked at your file was me a few months ago."

"Maybe someone didn't look at the file?"

"Let me see if someone just did a search on your name." After a few more minutes, her answer was the same as before. "No, that's empty too. Nobody's searched your name in months."

"Is it possible they could have kept that hidden?"

"No, it would still be logged. There would be a computer timestamp. They'd have to do a whole lot of hacking to erase that, and the security computers would have picked it up that something unusual was happening. There are safeguards against that sort of thing."

"So you're saying it's not you."

"Mike, would I lie to you?"

"Well, I would hope not. I thought we had built up some goodwill."

"We have. And I wouldn't throw that away."

"So it's someone else."

"If there's somebody after you... it's someone else."

"All right, thanks. Appreciate you getting back to me so fast."

"No problem. If you need anything else, let me know. I'll do what I can for you."

After putting his phone down, Recker looked at the others. They already knew what the answer was based on what they were hearing.

"So she says it's not them?" Jones asked.

"That's what she says."

"Do you believe her?" Mia asked.

Recker nodded. "I do."

Jones scratched the top of his head. "Well if we believe her, and we believe it's not Vincent, and we don't believe it's The Scorpions, then what do we have? We have eliminated all of our suspects."

Recker leaned back in his chair and put his hands over his eyes. He wished he could just go to sleep and wake up later with the problem already resolved. He knew it didn't work that way, though.

"Either we're way off base with our theories," Haley said. "Or someone's not as trustworthy as we think they are."

"Maybe you should ask Vincent point blank," Mia said.

"Wouldn't do any good. If it was him, he would deny it anyway."

"Well you could say the same thing about the CIA too."

Recker sighed. "Yeah, I guess you could."

"What this comes down to is we're going to need some proof," Jones said. "Until we have something definitive, everything else is just going to be wild speculation and guesswork."

"That's what we need. Proof. And we ain't got it."

"Not yet. But we will."

"I wish I had your confidence."

"So what are we going to do until then?" Mia asked. "Find another place to live?"

"I'm sorry. That's all we can do."

Mia's shoulders slumped. She knew Recker was right before, about a home being wherever they were together, but she couldn't help but be a little sad. It was their first place together. She was upset that they'd have to leave it under such circumstances.

"You guys can stay with me until you get situated," Haley said. "You know I got that extra bedroom. Stay as long as you want."

Mia looked at him and smiled. "Thank you." She turned back to Recker. "We still have our clothes and stuff though."

"Chris and I will go back, pack all our stuff, bring it with us."

"Why can't I go?"

Recker shook his head. "Not without knowing what's out there. Who knows if someone's watching or waiting? I'm not gonna take a chance and put you in danger."

"I hate this. I hate all of it."

Recker put his arms around her. "I know. So do I. I promise I'll get to the bottom of it, though."

"What if we get to Chris' and somebody's waiting for us there too?"

"They're not."

"How can you be sure?"

"Well, the way it looks right now is that they're only after me."

Mia pulled away from her boyfriend and looked at him with a terrifying thought. "You know, I just thought of something. What if you're right about everyone and none of them tried to kill you?"

"What are you getting at?"

"What if the shot wasn't meant for you? Maybe it was meant for me?"

Recker smiled. "Mia, I love you. But, seriously, you're a pediatric nurse at a hospital. Who'd be trying to kill you?"

Mia shrugged. "I don't know. I'm just trying to throw some possibilities out there."

"Well, I think you're throwing them too far out there."

"So you don't think I'm the target?"

"Uh, I would have my doubts."

"Oh. OK."

"It's good to think outside of the box sometimes," Recker said. "But I think it's safe to assume I'm the one they're after. And that's the way I would prefer it, anyway."

"Why?"

"Because I can live with me being the target. If it was you it'd drive me crazy."

Mia gave Recker a hug. "How long are we going to have to deal with this?"

Recker rubbed her back as he hugged her. "Not long. I promise."

4

Recker and Haley got everything they needed from the apartment and took it to Haley's place, where Recker and Mia spent the night. It was probably where they would be spending the next week or two until they found another apartment. With Recker trying to find out who was after him, that would likely be Mia's job, though on this day, she had to go to work. Recker dropped her off at the hospital, not wanting to take the chance of her going in alone. He feared that if someone was after him, and he knew where Mia worked, there might be a kidnapping job in there somewhere. He wanted to make sure she got there and didn't have to worry about her safety while he wasn't there. He even walked into the hospital with her to make sure she got to her floor.

Satisfied that she was safe, Recker went to the office, where Jones and Haley were already waiting for them. Jones immediately swiveled his chair around, hardly able to contain himself with the news.

"We found him."

Recker rushed over to the computer, where he saw a picture of a man leaning out of a car window. It was the same car that was used the day before to take a shot at him. There was no mistaking that car.

"That's him," Recker said.

"Are you sure this is the vehicle?" Jones asked.

"No doubt. That's it. Who is it?"

Jones reached down and grabbed a piece of paper he printed out. He handed it to Recker. "His name is Justin Sadko."

"Don't know him." Then Recker took his eyes off the paper. "Wait a minute. That name sounds familiar. Why do I know it?"

"Keep reading and you'll get your answer."

Recker kept reading, seeing that Sadko did have a criminal history. It was mostly small stuff. But the face looked familiar. He knew he'd seen it before. He just couldn't place it. Then he saw it.

"Vincent."

Jones nodded. "Currently affiliated with Vincent's crew, and has been for the last five years."

"That's why I know him. I've seen him here or there, though I don't think I've ever spoken to him. I've just seen the face, though I don't think I've seen it lately. Now it rings a bell. When we first started running down the list on Vincent's guys, I remember he was on the list. He's not high up in the organization though from what I gather."

"No, but perhaps that's changing."

"Could be this is something to change his stripes," Haley said.

Recker sighed and plopped down in a chair as he continued reading the rundown on Sadko. He then shook his head. He thought he had a better handle on his relationship with Vincent. How could he have been this wrong? It still didn't make sense to him, though. He could have thought of a hundred better ways Vincent could have taken him out if that's what he wanted.

Recker put the paper back down on the desk after he was finished and took a deep breath. "It still doesn't make sense."

"There is something peculiar about this," Jones said.

"I mean, not to toot my own horn here, but killing me would kind of be a big deal, no?"

"It would."

"So in theory, if Vincent wanted me dead, who would he send after me? His best guy, right? His most trusted guy?"

"Yes."

"So who is that?"

"Malloy," Haley replied.

"Exactly," Recker said. "So why wouldn't he send him instead of this guy who's not even high on the totem pole?"

"Maybe it's a test for him?" Jones asked.

Recker glanced at him like he said something ridiculous. "You really think I'd be the guy you send someone on a test for? I don't think he could take the chance of a fail, which is what happened. And why would it be just me? He'd still have to contend with you two. He knows you exist."

"Maybe he doesn't think we're as much of a threat," Haley said.

"But he knows you are. He's not dumb. And we all know how Vincent operates. He's not a guy who rushes in before he's ready. This thing seems kind of sloppy. Look at all the times we've done business with him. Or with the Scorpions even. Vincent will wait until the right opportunity, when the time is right, when the time suits him. He doesn't rush because he doesn't want to make mistakes."

"So maybe this guy is acting without Vincent's knowledge."

Recker looked at Jones for his thoughts. "Well?"

"It would certainly be a possibility," Jones replied. "It does seem like a somewhat unusual pattern for Vincent to partake in."

"We need to figure out what's going on here."

"How do you intend to do that? Other than finding Mr. Sadko here."

"Go right to the source."

"I infer that to mean you intend to talk to Vincent about it?"

Recker smiled. "Yep."

"Are you sure that's wise?"

"I can usually tell if someone's lying to me. I may not always be able to tell what they're covering up, or what they're hiding, but I can usually tell if it's not the truth."

"So what's the plan?" Haley asked.

Recker shrugged. "Only got one. Call him and find out."

Recker pulled out his phone right away and called Malloy, who picked up on the second ring.

"Hey, what's up?"

"Need to talk to the bossman," Recker answered.

"He's really busy today. Has a lot of meetings."

"You need to unbusy him. Now."

"Sounds urgent."

"It is."

"What's going on?"

"I need to know something. And I need to know it from him."

"And you need it today?"

"I do. If not, I may start making some assumptions that may not be accurate."

"Sounds like we're talking about a dire situation."

"We are. There's something big happening. And I need to know what's going on."

"I'll, uh, talk to him and call you back in a few minutes."

"OK."

"If he can make it, I assume it'll be at the usual place."

"No," Recker said. "I'll pick the place. And I'll pick the time."

Malloy could tell by his words that something big was going on. "I'll relay the message."

It didn't take even five minutes for Recker to get that return phone call.

"Boss says he can meet you in one hour. Where?"

"Love Park. I don't wanna see anyone else there except for him. And you. The rest of his guys have to stay on the outside."

"You sound like this meeting is a prelude to a war or something."

"Maybe it is."

"Something happen that I'm not aware of?"

"I don't know. We'll see when you get there."

Recker hung up, then looked at his partners.

"Love park?" Jones said. "Interesting choice."

"Wherever I meet with him, I want it to be public. Out in the open. Less chance of anything happening."

"Afraid your instincts about him are not correct?"

Recker shrugged. "It has occurred to me that it's possible he orchestrated the other hit, knowing it would fail, or wanting it to fail, knowing that I would reach out to him and call this meeting. Maybe that's what he was hoping for. Drawing me in for a better opportunity."

"But you don't really believe that."

"No. But I can't say it hasn't crossed my mind."

"So what's your plan here?"

"Well, meeting time is in an hour. So we need to get down there."

"We?"

"Me and Chris. If I'm wrong, I want some backup there."

"Works for me," Haley said.

"So you're gonna need to figure out a spot you can cover me from. Unobstructed."

"And unobserved I take it?"

"That too. And you're gonna have to find one fast. I want you to be looking out from wherever you are and letting me know if you find something that doesn't add up."

"Like men where there shouldn't be?"

"Exactly."

"Let's get to it."

Recker and Haley grabbed their guns and went out the door, hopping in different cars as they traveled to downtown Philadelphia. Love Park was officially known as the John F. Kennedy Plaza, located near City Hall, and an entrance for the Benjamin Franklin Parkway. It was nestled between 15th and 16th streets and Arch Street. It got its nickname from the iconic LOVE statue designed by Robert Indiana in 1976. There was a big water fountain in the middle of it, to go along with a grassy area, open paved areas, as well as walking paths, benches, and tables for eating. The park also sometimes served festivals and events in the area. It was a popular spot amongst tourists and locals alike, many of whom liked to take pictures standing by the LOVE sculpture.

Recker and Haley got there about twenty minutes before the scheduled meeting time. It didn't give them a lot of time to set up. Recker quickly found an open table. Haley was not as lucky. There were plenty of buildings around, but finding an open room, or an uncovered rooftop that couldn't be seen from other nearby buildings would be too much of a challenge in a short amount of time. With a hat pulled low to conceal his face, Haley walked around the perimeter of the park.

"I'm gonna have to cover you from the street. There's not enough time for anything else."

"That's fine," Recker replied. "As long as you can see what's going on."

"I can. You'll be good."

They didn't have to wait the full twenty minutes for the meeting to begin. Vincent showed up ten minutes later. His was among three cars that pulled up. He got out, along with Malloy, and started walking into the park. Several more of his men got out, though they stayed back towards the street. Recker immediately picked them up and watched their movements closely.

"You got them?"

"I see them," Haley said. "Nothing unusual so far."

"Keep alert."

Though the park was pretty active with a fair amount of people in it, Vincent and Malloy quickly spotted Recker. He was the only one sitting by himself. They walked over to his table and sat down across from him.

"Thanks for coming," Recker said.

"Judging by the urgency that this meeting was requested, it didn't seem like I had much choice," Vincent said.

"Well there's always a choice. It just depends on which door you wanna walk through."

"So what's this about?"

"Someone took a shot at me yesterday."

"Oh? First I've heard of it."

"I was just walking on the street somewhere, with someone else, not on the job."

"And someone just happened to recognize you?"

"Seemed strange to me too."

"And what, you think I had something to do with it?"

"It occurred to me. I also went back to my house and found someone had broken into it. Left a mess all over."

"Mike, I give you my word it wasn't me. Why would I do that?"

"I don't know. That's what I'm trying to find out.

There's only a select group of people that would have the resources to do that."

"And I'm at the top of the list."

"Second, actually," Recker said with a smile. "The first one checked out already."

"Mike, I swear I would never do that. I wouldn't even attempt to follow you. I know you're too good for that."

"There's also the possibility of following someone who's close to me. And we both know you already know who that is and where she works. I've trained her well. But maybe she tripped up somewhere along the line."

Vincent put his hand up. "Mike, as God is my witness, I have not, and would not, lift a finger against you. I thought we've built up enough trust over the years for us to know better."

"I thought so too. Then we found this."

Recker reached into his pocket and removed the picture of Sadko. He placed it down on the table for his guests to see. Vincent picked it up and looked at it. It was obvious from his face that he wasn't pleased with what he was seeing.

"What is this?" Vincent asked.

"This is the man that took the shot."

Vincent looked up from the picture and stared at Recker. "You're sure?"

"Positive."

"Since we're here, I'm assuming you've already made the connection and identified him."

"Justin Sadko. I believe he works for you."

Vincent handed the picture off to Malloy, who also had a displeased look on his face as he stared at the photo.

"I can see why this was so urgent for you," Vincent said.

"You can see how it looks," Recker replied.

"I do. It makes it seem as if I may be behind this."

"A little bit."

"Crumb," Malloy whispered.

"What?"

"Not you. Stinking Sadko bum. If I get him in front of me, I'll kill him myself."

Vincent put his hand on Malloy's arm. "Easy, Jimmy. As you may be able to deduce, Mr. Sadko is no longer part of my employment."

"As of today, or is this a longer-term thing?"

"As of three months ago."

"So this wasn't with your blessing?"

Vincent put his arms out as if he were going to give Recker a hug. "Mike, after all the things we've been through together. Do you really think I would try to gun you down on a street corner? Even if we were on the outs, which I want to stress that we're not, but even if we were, I would give you more dignity than gunning you down on the street with all the other slobs out there."

"So if you didn't send him, what's the story with this guy?"

"He's been with me for five or six years now. Or was I guess I should say. Wasn't a bad hand. But he had some reliability issues. With the time he'd put in, he thought he should've been higher up in the food chain. With the issues he had, I resisted until I could trust him more."

"What kind of reliability issues?"

"Showing up on time, being a few minutes late, not being where he's supposed to be, things like that. In our business, a few minutes late on some deals can cause a million dollars to go up in smoke."

"So what, you got rid of him?"

"No. Because I liked him, I wanted to try to work with him to correct his issues. Develop him. He got tired of waiting, I guess. A few months ago he said he was leaving to pursue other opportunities, and I gave him my blessings."

"Did you know those other opportunities involved killing me?"

"I swear I did not. If I did, I would've taken care of him myself."

"How did he find out where I lived?"

"That I don't know. Perhaps he followed the missus home from work one day? Or maybe he followed you from one of our meetings? I don't know."

"Know where he lives?"

"I did. I would doubt he is still there, though."

"I'm gonna need everything you have on him."

"You'll get it. I would suggest you let me take care of him, though. This is a stain on me."

"With all due respect, I'm the one he tried to kill. If you wanna look for him, go ahead. But I'm not stopping until I see him in a bag."

"Understood."

"What's the purpose of him coming after me, anyway?"

"If I had to guess, I would say he's trying to make a name for himself."

"He planning on taking you on?"

"I would think that's just crazy talk at this point. But after him trying to kill you, maybe that's what he is now. When he left, he said he wanted to pursue some other opportunities elsewhere. I assumed that meant he was leaving the city. It now appears that was a misguided assumption."

"Seems like they're coming out of the woodwork lately."

"If you're referring to challenges for me, it's just part of the deal. When you get to the top like me, there's always going to be someone vying for that spot. The Italians, Jeremiah, Nowak, the Scorpions, rogue cops, Justin, it's always something. There's always someone looking for a slice of the pie."

"Get tiresome?"

"It is what it is. I could ask the same question of you."

43

"Could."

"And?"

"I'd probably give you the same answer. It is what it is. So do you think this Sadko has other guys with him?"

"I'd like to say he's alone, but I think that would be wishful thinking. He's had three months to acquire and integrate men into his group. I'm sure he's taken advantage of that time. He has learned under me, after all."

Vincent was reading Recker's face, as he always did, looking for underlying clues in his feelings that weren't being conveyed with his words. This was one of those times where he was holding something back.

"What else is there?" Vincent asked. "I hope this hasn't strained our relationship. I give you my word this was done without my knowledge or blessing."

"You can't control people who aren't with you anymore. I get that."

"But?"

Recker looked away, noticing a younger couple posing for pictures by the LOVE statue. "Mia."

"Was she with you when the attempt took place?"

"She was. And she knows about the apartment being broken into."

"I'm sure that must have her rattled some."

"It does."

Vincent continued reading Recker's face. He thought he knew where he was coming from. "And now you're worried that he knows where she works and may use her to get to you."

"I guess it's crossed my mind."

"How 'bout stashing her somewhere?" Malloy asked.

Recker shook his head. "Won't work. Yeah, for a day or two, maybe, but if it takes longer than that, she won't go for it. She's stubborn. She's not gonna be deterred from living her life and working."

Without hesitation or thought, Vincent came up with a plan. "Then let me give you some peace of mind."

"How's that?"

"I feel some responsibility for this whole thing since he used to work for me. Allow me to set up protection for her."

"In what way?"

"I'll put men at the hospital around the clock. Or at least whenever she's working. I'll put a man inside and one on every entrance and exit possible. I'll make sure she's not bothered. My men will know what to look for."

"How will you know when she's there?"

"Just give me her schedule. I'll arrange everything."

"Hey," Malloy said. "I didn't help rescue her from a hospital just to let her fall into the hands of some psycho that used to work for us. I'll take care of the details. You know I will."

Recker was inclined to believe them. Especially

Malloy. He thought they had forged something that he could trust.

"What about a tail?" Recker asked.

"Let us know what you want," Vincent asked. "If you wanna pick her up at the hospital? Or if you want her to meet you somewhere? You name it, we'll make sure she gets there."

Recker nodded, about to take them up on their offer. At least that way he knew Mia would be taken care of while he was off hunting Sadko.

"How long is this offer good for?"

"For as long as it takes," Vincent answered.

"I give you my word," Malloy said. "I'll protect Mia until this son of a bitch is dead and buried. And that's a promise."

5

Recker and Haley went back to the office after meeting with Vincent. Recker retold everything that Vincent and Malloy said, as well as what they were offering. Everyone seemed to be on board with it, except for one.

"Do we really have to do this?" Mia asked. "I really don't want to ask him for protection."

"We didn't ask," Recker replied. "He offered."

"It's the same thing. I'm not really comfortable with knowing his men are watching my every move."

"They're not watching your every move. They're just going to watch the hospital and be on the lookout."

"How will they know if someone looks suspicious?" Jones asked.

"Maybe they're already aware of some of the guys that Sadko's recruited," Haley answered.

Recker pointed at him. "Yeah, that could be. Anyway, if there's anyone who would know if something doesn't look right, it's them."

"It still makes me uncomfortable," Mia said. "What if they're lying to you?"

"They're not."

"How do you know?"

"It's like they pointed out. They didn't help me get you out of that hospital a few months ago just to change their minds now. If they wanted me, or you, out of the way, they could have easily turned on us there."

"They had reasons not to then."

"Malloy took a bullet in helping to get you out of there."

"So does that make you besties now?"

"No, but I don't think he'd lie to me now."

"You put too much faith into these people."

"And you don't put enough. It's like when Chris and I worked at the CIA. You don't always work with friends. Sometimes your ally today is someone you wouldn't trust under normal circumstances. But your goals align together for a common purpose. That's all it is. Our goal and Vincent's goal align together."

"I think that's only because he doesn't want to go up against you and as long as you are somewhat on good terms, you'll look the other way with the things that he does."

"There might be some truth to that. But as long as

he sticks to his business and isn't hurting innocent people, I can live with that."

"So you really think this is a good idea?"

"I think it's the best idea we have at the moment."

"So how is this gonna work?"

"Whenever you have to work, I'll drop you off, then I'll pick you up when you're done. It'll save some time of you meeting me at some other secret location and then driving around for a while trying to lose any possible tails, and then finally going home. This way we can skip a few steps."

"What if you're busy whenever I'm done?"

"If it's small, Chris can handle it. And if it's not, we'll figure it out."

Mia sighed, still not liking it, though she knew it was probably for the better. And it was probably as good a plan as they had. "I really hope this doesn't take long."

"I hope not too." Recker then turned to Jones. "How are we looking on that front?"

"Working on it," Jones replied. "Like everything, it will take some time. I assume this man has spent the last three months building up his organization if he has one."

"Speaking of which," Haley said. "What exactly is the point of all this? I mean, what's the beef with you? Why do this?"

Recker shook his head, not sure if he had an answer. At least not one that was based on any facts.

"Unless it really is as simple as this guy wanting to make a name for himself. What better way to announce your arrival than by taking me out?"

"He could do that by taking out Vincent, who he probably knows better than you and could plan for that better."

"Maybe he figures he doesn't have enough men for that. He saw me, thought I was an easy target, made his move. Could be as simple as that."

"If that's the case, then I don't think this guy's playing with all his marbles. Sounds like he's got a screw loose."

"Nobody said he was playing with a full deck."

"He might not even be playing with half a deck."

"I guess we'll find out."

Recker then pulled out his phone and started making a call.

"Who are you calling?" Jones asked.

"Getting all hands on deck."

"What does that mean?"

Recker started talking into the phone. "Tyrell, need you to get ears on the street for me."

"What's shakin'?"

"I need you to find out all you can about a Justin Sadko."

"Radko?"

"No, Sadko. Used to be in Vincent's operation. I'm sure you ran into him over the years."

"Hmm. Don't ring a bell off-hand. The name don't

really strike me. Maybe I'd recognize him if I saw a picture."

"Well I can send you one if you want."

"Might be helpful. What do you want this dude for?"

"He tried to kill me yesterday."

"Say what?"

"You heard me."

"He really tried to off you?"

"Yep."

"Does Vincent know about this?"

"He does."

"Then why not just let him take care of it? Because you know Vincent ain't gonna stand for his guys taking jobs off the books and working without his orders and his A-OK. He'll kill the guy himself for a stunt like that."

"Sadko doesn't work for Vincent anymore," Recker said. "Left around three months ago."

"Oh. So what's he after you for?"

"Who knows? Maybe he's looking to make a name for himself. Or maybe I saw him at a meeting once and gave him an evil eye. Like I said, who knows? He also found out where I live and wrecked my apartment."

"Dang, man, that's messed up."

"Tell me about it. Anyway, I'll send you his picture. I don't really have anything else on him right now so if you can get the ball rolling and find out something I'd appreciate it."

"You got it, man, I'll start digging today. I'll see what I can come up with for you."

"Thanks." Recker then turned to everyone. "Well, Tyrell's on the job."

"So where does that leave us?" Mia asked.

"Well, we got you protection for when I'm not there. We got Vincent looking for this guy. We got Tyrell looking for this guy. We're looking for this guy. Between the three of us, we're the best in the city. We'll find the guy."

Jones continued on with his typing, Mia joining him, doing what she could to help. Haley went over to the Keurig machine and poured himself some coffee. He motioned for Recker to come over and join him, looking like he wanted to keep it hush-hush. Recker did, also getting some coffee. He kept his back to the others while Haley looked at them, making sure they didn't hear what he was saying, though it was mostly Mia that he was trying to keep from hearing.

"There's something bothering me about this," Haley said, keeping his voice low.

"What's that?" Recker replied, also whispering.

"A lot of this makes sense, but some of it doesn't."

"Like what?"

"Like what they would be doing at your apartment. That part makes no sense to me. What's the point behind that?"

"I don't know. It's been bugging me too."

"I mean, they were obviously looking for something. And I doubt it was money or valuables or things like that. They were looking for something specific. Something they thought you had. There would be no point in breaking in unless they had something in mind. I mean, I doubt they wanted to just telegraph to you that they were there."

"I know," Recker said. "I just don't know what it could have been."

"So maybe there's more to this than just trying to kill you to put a notch on their belt. Maybe there's a more specific purpose in mind."

"Unless they were looking for clues about where else I might go. Here for instance. Or maybe they were looking for something that might indicate who you and David are, where you live, go, things like that. Maybe they thought I might have some papers lying around that would give them more things to go on."

"Could be. They missed their shot on the street. Maybe they thought they might not get another one. So they go to your apartment, ransack it, hoping to find an address, a name, something that would lead them to another place where they could take their next crack at it."

"Other than that, I don't know what they might have been looking for. Unless they were just trying to send a message. You know, the I know where you live type of thing. Trying to spook me out."

"They couldn't be stupid enough to believe something like that might work."

"A lot of it going around these days. I just hope we find this guy quickly. I don't know how much sneaking around Mia will be able to take."

"She's tough."

"I know. But it's not so easy when you're the one being hunted."

"Well it's not her."

"Might as well be. The way she's going to worry about me until this thing is settled, it's gonna hit her hard. It's one thing to do what we do. It's another when there's someone out there who's actually hunting us. Someone who knows where she works. Someone who knows where we live. That's the tough part."

Mia then turned around and looked at them. "What are you two mumbling about over there?"

"Oh, nothing. Just talking about which one of these coffee flavors we like best."

"I'm partial to all of them," Jones said.

Recker and Haley each brought them over a cup.

"What are you working on?" Recker asked.

"Just trying to see if I can trace Sadko's movements over the past couple of months," Jones answered. "Looking into phone records, credit cards, GPS's, things like that. Seeing if I can pick him up somewhere along the line."

"So can you?"

"It's hit and miss right now. I've got a few hits on him, but nothing concrete that we can establish a pattern from. And nothing recently. Everything is from two, three months ago."

"Cuts ties from Vincent, then drops off the grid," Haley said.

"Yeah," Recker said. "Question is whether this was his goal the whole time? Is this what he had in mind from the beginning when he left? Taking a shot at me?"

"Why wait so long if it was?"

"I don't know."

"My guess is that he has spent the last three months doing multiple tasks. One, acquiring more men, in the eventual phase that he takes on Vincent. Or at the very least begins to move in on Vincent and perhaps take away some of his territory."

"Vincent won't stand for that."

"I know. But Sadko won't be the first who has tried. And he won't be the last either."

"He has the one advantage that the others haven't had, though," Haley said. "He's been the only one who's been part of Vincent's organization. He'll know what Vincent likes to do, where he likes to go, what kind of strategies he uses, everything. Vincent would have to completely rethink his entire organization and plans to compensate for that."

"That's true," Recker said. "That would give Sadko the advantage."

"Besides all that," Jones said. "The second part of

his plan for the last three months, aside from acquiring more men, is to find you and take you out."

"But why?" Mia asked. "Just to give himself a bigger name?"

"It might be much more of a business calculation than that. He knows that at some point, he'll have to deal with you. It could be he was just trying to be proactive and eliminate you before you ever get to interfering with his plans."

"Could be," Recker said.

"Eliminate your enemy before he knows he is your enemy," Haley said. "Smart."

"It would be if he actually was able to carry it through. But he didn't. Now it's gonna be my turn. And when I get my shot... I won't miss."

6

Jones' lackluster demeanor instantly picked up. He sat up straighter and then leaned forward, almost as if he couldn't believe what he was seeing. He then reached over to a second computer and started typing away on that.

"What's going on?" Haley asked.

"You might be moving quickly soon," Jones answered.

"What's up?"

"Looks like we might have a home invasion commencing soon."

"How soon?"

"That's what I'm verifying now."

Haley looked at the time. "Mike should be on the way back now from dropping Mia off at the hospital."

"He'll have to meet you there."

"What are we dealing with?"

Jones scribbled a few things down on a piece of paper, then continued typing away. He switched between both computers and several screens on each one, printing several things out at once.

"Looks like we have got five people we're dealing with," Jones said. He took one of the printouts and handed it to Haley. "Get to that address now. It's going down in twenty minutes."

Haley quickly looked at it. "This place is at least twenty minutes away."

"That's why you've got to hurry."

Haley immediately grabbed a couple of weapons and then bolted out the door, hoping he could miraculously get to the place in time. With time being a factor, he had to look over the information Jones had given him while he was driving. There was definitely no time to study it and come up with a plan. He would just have to figure things out on the fly. And hope Recker could get there around the same time as him. Jones sent a text message to Recker, letting him know the urgency of the situation, as well as the address. Recker responded almost immediately. He was already on the way back from taking Mia to work, so he was a few minutes closer to the spot than Haley was.

The job was to protect a family in the suburbs of Newtown. There was a husband, wife, and two kids that lived there. They had now been targeted by a crew of thieves who had done some yard work for them previously and knew they were well off. Two of them had even been in the house before under the guise of using the bathroom. In reality, they used that cover to check the house out. While doing so, they knew there were some valuables in the house, including a safe. They also knew that the husband was high up in the pecking order of a technology company. None of the crew were safecrackers, so in order to get it open, they needed someone who knew the combination. That meant they had to break in by force and make someone open it for them. All five of the men had criminal records, though none of them would be considered hardened felons. None of them would be confused with choir boys either.

By the time Recker arrived on the scene, he could already see that he was too late. Too late to prevent it from happening, that is. Not too late to fix it. There was a white-colored van parked along the curb in front of the house. Looking at the two expensive looking cars in the driveway of the two-story house, and then looking at the dirty-looking van, it didn't take a genius to figure out that one didn't match the others. Though Recker didn't immediately see any doors or windows open, he knew the crew was in there.

He took out his gun and put the suppressor on, then snuck up to the side of the house, peeking in what wound up being the living room window. There was nobody in there. Going in through the front door didn't seem like the best idea, figuring they probably had someone on it. Recker went around the side of the house and opened the white vinyl gate. He went around to the back door, seeing double hung glass french doors. He kept his head down as he passed underneath a few windows.

Recker tapped on his earpiece. "Chris, how much time you got?"

"Give me a few minutes."

Recker then heard what sounded like a woman screaming. "Got trouble. Can't wait that long."

"I'm coming."

There were some curtains on the inside part of the french doors, but there was an open slit in the middle, allowing Recker to somewhat see inside. He still didn't see anyone. He pulled down on the handle of the door, and to his surprise, it opened. He would've gotten in even if it wasn't, but it did save a little time. He opened the door just enough for him to slip his body inside. He kept his gun out in front of him as he looked around and closed the door with his other hand. Then he heard another scream. It was coming from upstairs. Recker quickly ran through a hallway to get to the stairs. As soon as he turned the corner, though, he saw a man standing near the front door. He was armed with an assault rifle. As soon as the two men saw each other, they both instantly raised their weapons. Recker was quicker, though, and put two rounds in the man's chest before he was able to get off a shot. The man slumped to the floor. Recker stepped over his body as he started ascending the stairs.

Recker was about halfway up the steps when another man appeared at the top of them. He immediately saw Recker, who immediately saw him too. Just before the man was about to pull the trigger on his gun, a bullet ripped through his stomach, causing him to lose his balance and fall down the stairs. Recker moved to the side and clung to the wall as the man's body fell past him. Recker kept his eyes glued to the top of the stairs in case anyone else came strolling by. And he wasn't wrong. Upon hearing the thumping sound of one of their friends bumping down the steps, another one of the crew came by to see what was going on. After seeing Recker standing there, the next man immediately pointed his gun at him and fired before Recker was able to stop him. Recker ducked his head, the bullet whizzing past him and lodging into the wall. Recker returned fire, hitting the man in the left shoulder. He was just wounded, though. Recker raced up the rest of the steps to get to the man before he could revive himself. As Recker got to the top step, the man tried to sit up and reached for his weapon again. Recker put another bullet in him to end the contest.

He didn't know for sure, but Recker was pretty positive that everyone else in the house knew he was there. There were too many bodies thumping on the floor to spring a surprise on anybody else. Now on the second floor, Recker peeked his head around the wall to see which direction he should go in. The others came from the right, but that didn't mean everyone was there. And it didn't mean the occupants of the house were there either. They could have been split up. He then heard a noise coming from the right-hand side, and that was the direction Recker was going in. He walked past a bathroom, then down a short hall-way, before coming to a closed door.

Knowing the assailants were likely behind that door, and probably waiting for him to open it so they could blow his head off, Recker got down on the floor. Whenever the door opened, whoever was shooting at him would have their eyes up higher, expecting someone to be standing up. Him being on the ground would give him the advantage. At least for a second or two. And in this business, the advantage of a second or two was sometimes the difference between life and death.

The door was slightly ajar, though Recker couldn't see through the slit between the door and the frame. It just wasn't closed tightly. He then put his left hand on the bottom of the door and forcefully pushed it open. Almost immediately the shots came fast and furious. But they all were flying over his head, where the men expected Recker's body to be. Recker immediately located the first guy, almost directly in front of him. Two shots to the chest quickly eliminated him. Recker then looked further inside the room, and to the right, was what he assumed was the last remaining member of the team. Jones did say it was only a five-man group, and Recker took out four already.

Recker stood up and looked at the man, who now was hiding behind the woman that lived there, holding her as a hostage. He had a gun pointed at the side of her head. Recker glanced around at the rest of the room, making sure there were no more armed men, and also looking for the rest of the family. There was only the husband, though.

"Where are the kids?" Recker asked.

"They're at school," the woman answered.

"Shut up!" the man said, tugging at the woman's hair.

"You got nowhere to go," Recker said. "Might as well drop the gun and get out of here."

"No. You drop the gun and get out of here or I'll blow this woman's brains out."

"You do that and there's nothing that's keeping you from me. You kill her and I'll put a bullet in your head."

"Looks like we're in a standoff then."

"I can do this all day. How about you?"

The man took a deep breath, trying to think of a way he could get out of it. In reality, he was just trying to buy an extra minute or two. There actually a sixth man to the group, one that Jones hadn't detected. He was in another part of the house and was now sneaking his way towards Recker's position. The man was slowly creeping up the steps, trying not to make any noises or sounds, hoping that the stairs didn't creek as he went up them. He successfully made it to the top of the stairs, standing on the second to the top step, taking a few deep breaths before he jumped out at Recker and surprised him. The man jumped out from behind the wall and onto the top step, ready to fire into Recker's back. The shot rang out and Recker turned around to face the man. He was already on his way to the ground, though. With Recker turning around, the man holding the woman let go of her and took aim at Recker. He fired, but when Recker turned to face the other man, he squatted down, making this shot go high and over his head. Recker then spun back around to face him, hitting him square in the chest. As the man fell over, Recker quickly went over to the man who was now face down in the hallway. He peeked down the steps and saw Haley standing there.

"Looked like you could use some help."

Recker smiled, then laughed. "Just a little."

"Is that it? We done?"

"Looks that way."

Haley began walking around the house, just to make sure there was nobody else there. While he was doing that, Recker went back over to the man he just shot, making sure he was dead. Once he confirmed that he was, he went over to the husband and untied him. His wife ran over to him and hugged him.

"Thank you," the wife said. "Thank you so much."

Recker looked at them and nodded. "You're welcome."

"How did you guys get here so fast?" the husband asked.

"Huh?"

"You're cops, right? One of our neighbors call?"

"Uh, no, your neighbors didn't call."

"Then how'd you know?"

"We just got a tip. Everyone all right?"

"Yeah, we're fine," the wife answered. "Thank you again."

"Just you two in the house?"

"Yes, thankfully. Our kids are at school."

"Good. Well, we'll be going now. You guys take care."

"Wait," the husband said. "What do you mean, you're going? Don't you have to do some crime scene stuff or something?"

"Uh, no, we're not that type of police. We're more like an independent task force type of team. We just do what we have to do and leave. The regular cops do all that type of stuff."

"Oh. Well are they coming?"

"I would suggest calling them as soon as we leave."

"You guys don't do it?"

"No, they don't really like hearing from us."

"Oh."

"You guys take it easy."

Recker then left, leaving the husband and wife to look at each other, confused about what was happening.

"What do we do now?" the wife asked.

The husband shrugged. "I guess we call 911."

Recker went down the steps and found Haley standing by the front door, keeping a lookout outside.

"Everything good?"

"Clear as can be," Haley answered. "Sorry I got here so late."

"Your timing was perfect as far as I'm concerned. Let's head back to the barn, huh?"

They drove back to the office, only telling Jones that the mission was successful. Recker wanted to wait until he saw him in person to razz him a little bit. Once they got there, Recker only dropped a hint, wanting to drag it out a little.

"Everything went well then?" Jones asked.

"Oh yeah," Recker answered. "Six victims. But it was a success."

Jones immediately stopped typing, though he didn't turn around or say anything yet. He just sat there with his fingers on the keyboard, trying to decipher what he just heard. He then spun his chair to the side as he saw Recker and Haley getting a drink from the refrigerator.

"What do you mean, six victims? I thought you said it was a success."

"It was," Recker said.

"Well then why is there an extra body? Don't tell me one of the homeowners died before you got there?"

"Nope. Everyone was alive when I got there."

"You were too late to save them?"

"No, the homeowners are fine. They're both alive and kicking. No injuries. No physical ones anyway. Mentally is another story. Hard to get over something like that."

"Well then I don't understand what you are saying. If there were five perpetrators and there were six victims, and the homeowners are fine, and you're both fine, where did the other victim come from?"

"There weren't five of them," Recker replied. "There were six."

Jones looked at him like he had two heads. "What do you mean, six?"

"Uh, just what I said. There were six guys. Not five."

Jones looked at Haley. "Is he serious?"

"He is," Haley answered. "And he's correct. There were six."

"That's impossible." Jones immediately started typing away again. "There was nothing indicating a sixth man."

"Looks like maybe you screwed up a little," Recker said.

"Impossible. I was very clear and I double check everything three times before giving it to you."

"Maybe your system had a malfunction."

"My system is working perfectly."

"Looks like you finally screwed the pooch on this one."

Jones continued looking over his notes. "There is

nothing here that indicates a sixth man was even remotely in the cards."

"David, it's fine. Just because that sixth guy that I didn't know about or plan for almost killed me, it's no big deal."

"What?"

"It's nothing."

Jones started looking frantically at his notes, afraid he missed something that he shouldn't have. Recker looked at Haley and smiled. He had successfully worked Jones into a lather. His mission was done.

"David, it's fine, I'm just trying to mess with you."

Jones took a deep breath. "Thank goodness. I really thought I may have missed something. So there wasn't a sixth man, then?"

"Oh, there was a sixth man."

"There really was," Haley said.

Jones immediately went back to his notes, drawing a laugh from Recker. "David, it's fine. Really. Don't worry about it."

"How can you say not to worry about it?" Jones replied. "If I almost got you killed, then I must have screwed up somewhere along the way. Missed something."

"I'm sure you didn't miss anything. At the last minute they probably decided to bring someone else on board. Or maybe it was a friend or relative that they wanted to see if they would be a good fit for the group on a future job. Or maybe they just had someone tag along at the last minute. Could have been anything. It happens."

"But it doesn't happen to me. I make sure that I am quite thorough in explaining what you may come up against."

"And you do a great job of it. This isn't on you. Don't worry about it. Things happen out there that we can't account for or plan for. We all know that. Just part of the job. Besides, everything worked out. Bad guys went down, good guys are alive, homeowners are safe. Win all the way around."

Recker's phone went off, indicating a text message. Reading his body language, Haley could see that it wasn't something normal.

"Something wrong?"

"No, not really. Tyrell says he's got a guy who knows Sadko. Says he's willing to talk to me."

"Well that's good news," Jones said.

"Maybe."

"Why wouldn't it be?"

"I dunno. Just hesitant about walking into a trap I guess."

"Tyrell wouldn't do that," Haley said.

"It's not Tyrell that I'm worried about. How do we know this guy isn't playing him? Sadko worked for Vincent. He probably knows I have a relationship with Tyrell too."

"So he could have someone have Tyrell accidentally find them, which lures me in, then try a second attempt to finish what they started."

"Could be."

"So what do you plan on doing?" Jones asked.

"Same thing I always do," Recker replied. "Go in with my eyes wide open." Then he looked at Haley and pointed at him. "And a backup plan."

7

The man that was willing to talk to Recker initially wanted to meet at a park, but Recker put the kibosh on that. He wasn't talking to anybody in a wide open area. Too many variables that he couldn't control or know about at the moment. He wound up agreeing to meet the man at a small pub, that way Recker could see everything around him. Tyrell agreed to stay with the man until Recker got there.

Before going into the pub, Recker and Haley looked around outside for twenty minutes to make sure there was nobody out there with a gun waiting for them to come back outside. They didn't see anyone or suspect anything was amiss, not that it still couldn't happen. But it seemed legit so far.

"You know, Sadko may know my face now too if he was in on some of the stuff we did together," Haley said.

"Yeah, I know."

"So me slipping in there undetected may not work if he does."

Recker shrugged. "What other choice do we have?"

Recker and Haley went in, immediately splitting paths. Recker walked to the back of the room, instantly finding Tyrell, who stood up to make himself noticeable once he saw his friend walk in. Haley ordered himself a drink, then walked over to the side of the room and leaned against the wall. He would have looked out of place if he just stood there without anything in his hand.

"Mike, what's happening?" Tyrell said, shaking hands. He then looked over at the other guy, who Recker quickly glanced over to size up.

Though Recker didn't let his guard down, he didn't think he had a lot to worry about with this guy. At least not from him physically. If he was setting him up for something later, well, that was still a worry. But he didn't have to worry about this guy lunging over the table with a knife or anything. The man looked to be in his late forties, early fifties, and appeared to be a little down on his luck. His clothes were dirty and a little torn. He had one of those Newsboy Caps on that honestly looked a bit too big for his head. Recker figured the man probably found it on the street or behind a dumpster or something.

"This is J.J.," Tyrell said.

Recker and J.J. shook hands, then sat down. They all had drinks in front of them, including Recker.

"Took the liberty of getting one for you," Tyrell said.

"Thanks."

"You can bring Chris on over if you want, man, this is all on the up and up. You ain't gotta worry about J.J. He's good people."

"I like to be sure."

"I know. But I'd have given you a heads-up if I thought there was something hinky about this."

"So you're The Man," J.J. said, looking a bit wild-eyed. He was kind of in awe, like he was meeting a sports hero or an actor or something.

"I don't know about that," Recker replied.

"You're a legend in this city, man. A man of the people. Always looking out for the little guy."

"I do my best."

"It's just an honor sitting down here at the same table as you, man. Just a real honor."

Recker couldn't help but let out a small smile. Well, half of one anyway. It was nice to hear those words, but it wasn't what he was there for. "What's this about Sadko? I hear you know him?"

"Know of him, man. Like, I don't know him like friends or anything. But I get around, you know?"

"So what do you know?"

"Listen, I'll be straight up upfront with you, man... I ain't exactly living the high life right now. I don't always know where I'll be sleeping, where my next meal's coming from, things like that. Money isn't exactly a friend to me, you know what I mean?"

"Sure."

"But one thing I do know... I hear things. I'm all over this city. And I hear things."

"What kind of things?"

"I hear that this Sadko dude is after you."

Recker was always appreciative of any information that he could get. But this wasn't exactly breaking news to him. He hoped this wasn't all that he was being brought down there for. Tyrell wouldn't have brought him if it was, though. He knew Tyrell wouldn't have asked him to come if it wasn't something important. Something that he could use.

"I hope you've heard more than that," Recker said. "I've already had a few bullets fly over my head. I already know he's after me."

"Yeah, but, he's one of Vincent's crew. At least used to be."

"I know."

"And he's been recruiting people hard all over this city these last couple months."

"Already figured that."

"Word on the street is that he's a few dollars short of a Lincoln, if you know what I mean?"

"Already figured that part out."

"Seems like I'm telling you a lot you already know."

"So far. Have anything else?"

"Well check this out, yo. What you may not know is, did you know that he's got something major planned for you later tonight?" Recker's eyes squinted. It was obviously not something he had heard. J.J. smiled and pointed at him, knowing he actually told him something useful. "Ahh, see, I knew I could say something you needed."

"Later tonight. What time?"

J.J. shrugged. "Don't know."

"How do you know this?"

"Heard two dudes talking."

"Where?"

"Uh, it was a little place off of Market Street. Little restaurant that's there. Not a big place, but sometimes if they got leftovers or whatever, they sometimes just put it back for whoever to take. You know, people down on their luck."

"And there just happened to be a couple of Sadko's men there talking about me?"

"Well no, not exactly."

"Then how exactly is it?"

"You see, what I do is, I take the food and put it in a bag, then I go over a couple streets and find a nice quiet place to sit down and relax and eat. And there was these two dudes talking there. They didn't know I was there, I guess. Or they didn't care. I don't know. But anyway, they were already talking by the time I got there."

"What were they saying?"

"Just about how Recker's girl works at such-and-such hospital. I never did get the name. Though I guess you know it, huh?" Recker nodded. "Yeah, then they said that they were gonna give her a surprise tonight, and it was something that would send you back reeling so hard you'd never recover."

Recker took his eyes off J.J. and looked at Tyrell, who simply gave him a look back. Recker hated hearing that Mia was a target because of him. It was something that had already happened too many times before. Now he had to figure out whether this guy was saying something he needed to hear or whether he was saying something Sadko wanted him to hear. A down on his luck guy like J.J. would say just about anything if someone slipped them a few bucks. Recker didn't get the vibe this was that kind of situation, though. But it was still something he had to consider.

"And you don't know a time? Early tonight? Late tonight?"

"Never said," J.J. answered. "At least not when I was listening."

"You hear anything else?"

"No, not really. They started looking around and as soon as they saw me, they split."

Recker reached into his pocket and pulled out two hundred dollars and slid it across the table. "Get yourself a place to stay for a few days and some clothes."

"Hey, thanks, man," J.J. happily said, picking up the

money. "You're a good dude, man. Not like them other guys."

"Why?"

"As they were leaving, one of them called me a bum. That ain't right, man. You shouldn't talk to someone like that. I ain't no bum. I might be down on my luck a little. But that don't give no one the right to say things like that."

"No, it doesn't." Recker stood up. "You take care of yourself, OK?"

"I will, man. You take care of your lady friend too, huh? Don't let anything happen to her."

"I won't."

Recker walked away from the table and found Haley against the wall. He explained everything that J.J. told him. Tyrell walked over only a few seconds later.

"Well what do you think?" Recker asked.

"The information is good, I think," Tyrell answered.

"How well you know this guy?"

"I've gotten some things from him before. They always turned out good. He's one of them guys who's always down on his luck. Been going on that way for him as long as I've known him."

"Which is how long?"

"Going on five years now, probably."

"And you think he's reliable?"

"If you're thinking he's a plant... I just don't see it. If

that's the direction Sadko was going, there's plenty of others guys I'd think about before J.J. I just don't see using him as the guy to spread false info like that."

"Well if Sadko knows you're with me, and he knows you know this guy, it's not a stretch for him to connect the dots."

Tyrell shook his head. "Nah, I don't think so. The connection to you and me, maybe. But there ain't no way he knows I know J.J."

"Sure about that?"

"Positive. I've never mentioned him to Vincent. He's not one of my main guys for info or anything. Just someone I check in on from time to time. I guarantee that there ain't no way that Sadko knows about him."

Recker looked at his partner. "What do you think?"

"I don't really see how we got much choice either way," Haley replied. "If he's telling the truth, we gotta go. We can't afford to choose the alternative and pass it off. And even if it's a setup, I don't see how we could sit it out, anyway. It'd still be a chance to knock off him or some of his men or find out what's going on. Seems like a pretty slam dunk choice no matter what. And if Tyrell's right that Sadko don't know the guy, seems our minds are already made up."

"Yeah, even if there was only a one percent chance that this was happening," Tyrell said. "You can't let your girl twist in the wind like that."

Recker nodded. "I agree. We're just gonna have to keep our heads up."

8

Recker and Haley were walking around the hospital, looking for anyone who looked like they might not belong. It was a tough chore to pick out a single person who may not have belonged in a building that literally had thousands of people in it. For all they knew, someone from Sadko's group could have been posing as a doctor or a hospital worker. It wouldn't take much effort to find a white coat somewhere to try to blend in.

After walking around the hospital for a few minutes, they met Malloy just in front of the cafeteria. Once Recker heard about the possible plan, he immediately called Vincent to have his men keep a close watch on things. Vincent did one better. He sent over ten more to parade inside the building.

"How you guys making out?" Malloy asked.

Recker shook his head. "Nothing on our end. You?"

"Same here."

"One thing's for sure," Haley said. "We're not gonna be able to keep on walking around this building indefinitely. Security's gonna pick up that we're not doing anything and just walking around aimlessly."

"We're not aimless," Malloy replied. "And don't even worry about it. Security's been taken care of."

"What? How?"

Malloy grinned. "It's like Vincent always says. It pays to have friends. Everywhere."

Recker rubbed his face and snickered. "He's even got someone on the security staff here, doesn't he?"

"There isn't anything anywhere that that man doesn't know about."

Recker shook his head. "I should've known. All this time Mia's been working here, and he's always had a guy on the inside."

"Don't worry about it, though. He's never used it to track your movements or hers. It's just something he's had in his back pocket should the need arise."

"That's why he was so confident about this."

"So you got someone watching the cameras right now?"

"We do."

"That must mean Sadko doesn't have anyone in the building yet," Haley said. "We would've found out by now."

"Maybe," Recker said. "Still gotta figure out what their angle is."

"If they have one," Malloy said. "This could all still be a wild goose chase."

"The guy was sure of what he heard."

"Maybe they just changed their minds."

"Could be."

"Let's look at it realistically, though," Haley said. "If they were gonna make a play on Mia, where would they do it? They wouldn't do it on the pediatric wing, too high profile. Locked doors, cameras, too tough to get in."

"That makes sense," Malloy said. "They'd have to wait till she was outside to grab her."

"If grabbing her is their intention," Recker replied. "Who knows what else they're thinking about."

"Even still, if her floor is off limits, then it's somewhere between the elevator and the front door."

Recker then looked in the window of the door to the cafeteria. "Or in there."

"So let's stop wasting our time then by walking around the building looking for this clown. Let's just concentrate on where someone would come and get her, and we let them come to us. We'll have her path covered from up there to down here completely. Somebody at each step of the way. Then when they make their play, we take them instead."

Just to make sure they hadn't overlooked anything, the three of them entered the cafeteria and made a sweep of the room. No one looked out of place, though. They were specifically looking for one, maybe two people, who were sitting by themselves, who didn't look like they might have been visiting someone or who might have worked there. There were only two people who were sitting by themselves, and judging by the fact that both of them looked to be in their seventies, they felt sure they could rule them out.

"Never know," Haley said. "Maybe Sadko's recruiting from everywhere."

"Not likely," Malloy replied. "I know that guy. And he's not recruiting anyone over the age of fifty."

"Why? He got some type of age discrimination thing going on?"

Malloy made a confusing type of face. "I dunno, he's got some weird thing going on in his head."

"I think we already figured that part out," Recker said.

"No, but I mean, really. He's got some type of issue thinking that once you reach a certain age, you can't do this type of job anymore."

"Really?"

"What, once you hit fifty you can't hold a gun and shoot straight?"

Malloy shrugged. "I'm telling you, man, the guy's got a screw loose. He's not all the way there."

"That why Vincent never promoted him?"

"Partially. It wasn't just the reliability thing like Vincent said. It was also because he had some really strange ideas, like the one I just said, and Vincent wasn't sure he could trust him in a leadership position.

Didn't trust he could make the right or tough call in a tough situation. He thought he might crumble."

"Great. It's bad enough we have to deal with people like this to begin with, then you throw in that they're crazy to boot?"

"Which also means the people he's recruiting aren't probably playing with a full deck either. Normal people aren't going to flock to him. They're gonna see that he's crazy and pass."

"Unless he's offering them something big," Recker said. "Like the opportunity to take me out. Or Vincent."

Malloy nodded. "Yeah."

"Well, let's start splitting up."

"Where do you wanna be in this?"

"I figure me and you take opposite sides of the cafeteria. Chris can take by the elevator she'd use to get off. Then you can spread your guys around. Put one on her floor near the elevator, then the rest spread out between Chris' spot and us."

Malloy walked a few feet away as he got on his phone to relay the orders to the rest of his men.

"What do you really think is gonna happen here?" Haley asked.

"I don't know," Recker replied.

"Seems like not the greatest plan here if this is Sadko's intention. A lot of risks. A lot of variables."

"Not if he thinks no one is here to prevent it. If we weren't here, what's the risk? And the one thing about dealing with someone like him is, it's tough to predict what he's going to do. What's normal doesn't apply to him. Everything's on the table."

Haley left, tapping Malloy on the shoulder as he walked by. After Malloy was done on the phone, he went back to Recker.

"All right, everything's set up. I got a guy on her floor now, watching the elevator. I doubt they'd do anything there though."

"I agree."

"Then Chris is on this floor and I got guys lined up along the way here. A couple look like nurses, hospital workers mopping floors and stuff. We got her protected."

"Put a guy on each floor down here too. Just in case they have designs of someone getting on at another floor, then also getting off on that floor."

"Yeah, good idea. I'll get them on it."

After Malloy successfully moved his people around, he and Recker went inside the cafeteria and waited. They each took up opposite sides of the room. They also each grabbed a newspaper, something to drink, and a small plate of food to try to blend in.

Malloy pretended to rub his ear while actually touching his earpiece. "Everybody on channel?"

Everyone checked in that they were. An hour passed by with no activity noticed by anyone.

"She just got on the elevator," one of Malloy's men said.

"This is it, boys," Malloy said. "If it's gonna happen, it's probably happening now. Stay sharp."

A minute later, Haley's voice was heard. "Mia just stepped off. Heading to the cafeteria now."

When she finally appeared in the cafeteria, Malloy picked her up. "All right, I got her."

As Mia was getting her food, she suddenly turned and looked around, getting a feeling that something wasn't right. She looked right at Malloy's position, who put a newspaper in front of his face to disguise himself since she knew what he looked like.

"She's on to something," Malloy said.

"I've taught her well," Recker replied. "She's probably caught a few things out of the corner of her eye that she knows isn't like normal. Just stay cool. If there's nothing obvious she'll go right to her table."

After Mia paid for her food, she went to the back of the cafeteria and sat down at a table. Recker and Malloy continued looking all around, waiting for that one thing to catch their eye. That one thing that was off.

"How's everything looking in the hallway?" Recker asked.

"Everything looks clear out here," Haley answered.

It only took about five minutes before the plan became clear. A taller man, probably in his early thirties, and wearing a white doctor's coat, approached Mia's table.

"May I sit?"

"Sure," Mia replied.

"Crap, who's that?" Malloy asked. "That guy work here?"

"Doesn't look familiar," Recker answered.

"If we go in and that guy's really a doctor, we'll blow everything."

"Just let it play out for a minute. If he starts taking her somewhere, we can still grab him before he walks out of here."

"So what unit are you in?" the doctor asked.

"Umm, pediatrics," Mia replied. "You."

"Well, I'm kind of in a new unit."

"Oh? What's that?"

"The kind that's gonna take you where I say. And you're gonna go with me or I'm gonna put a bullet in your stomach with the gun I've got hiding underneath the table."

"What?"

"Don't do anything strange. Don't make any sudden movements. And don't scream out. If you do any of those things, I'm gonna kill you right here. You understand?"

Luckily for Mia, or unluckily, she'd been through situations like this before. Unfortunately, as Recker always said, you get used to it. Someone who hadn't been through it might have panicked. But not her. There was not an ounce of panic going through her mind. Her immediate thoughts were about how she was going to get out of it. Just like Recker always taught her if something went wrong. The people that panicked wound up dead. The people that thought clearly and calmly, they figured a way out. They were the ones that survived.

"Yes. What did I do?"

"Doesn't matter."

Recker was looking at Mia's face and noticed the change in her expression. "Something's not right. She looks different."

"How?" Malloy asked.

"Tough to explain. She suddenly stopped eating and stiffened up. As if she'd just heard something troubling."

"Let's go in."

"Wait. I got another idea. I'll call her and see."

"Sure that's wise? What if she doesn't play it right?"

"She will," Recker said, confident in her abilities.

Recker took out his phone and called Mia. Mia's phone was in her pocket, but heard the ringer going off.

"I really should get that," Mia said.

"Leave it," the fake doctor replied.

"If I don't answer it, they'll know something's wrong."

"Fine. Answer it. But if you say one wrong word, I'll kill you before you can finish the conversation."

Mia nodded, then slowly took the phone out of her pocket. She saw it was Recker and hoped she would get an opportunity to say something that would let him know she was in trouble. She answered the phone, but Recker immediately started talking, not letting her get a word in.

"Hey, I need you to just listen to me and not say anything. Don't do anything sudden and don't say anything that'll give me away. I know there's a guy sitting across from you at your table."

Mia started to turn her head as if she were going to look for her boyfriend, then quickly stopped.

"I told you, no sudden moves. Just listen."

"Yeah, yeah, they just needed one more shot."

"I'm already here so you don't have to worry. Is that guy across from you a real doctor."

"Uh, no, I don't think I know that patient. What's the deal with him?"

"I don't know, but it sounds like a dangerous situation. Maybe if you sedate the patient first, that'll help."

"Does he have a gun?"

"The doctor said he did, but I don't know if he knew what he was talking about."

The man across from Mia put his finger in the air and started twirling it around, wanting her to wrap it up.

"OK, I've, uh, someone wants to talk to me about something so I have to go."

"We're coming."

Mia looked at the man and smiled, holding the phone up, feeling a lot more confident about her situation. "Thanks for letting me take that. It was really important."

Recker stood up. "He's our guy. Let's go."

Malloy also immediately got up and walked over to Mia's table. Mia saw Recker approaching and made sure not to give his position away by looking at him too long. She happened to look to her left and did a double take when she saw Malloy coming too. She put her eyes back on the man in front of her and coughed, making sure she gave them enough time to get to her before they got up.

"So are you gonna tell me what this is about?"

The man shrugged. "Someone wants me to bring you to them. That's all I know."

"This person have a name? Do I know them?"

"I dunno. And names are unimportant. All you gotta do is follow directions. If you do, maybe you'll actually come back in one piece."

"I doubt it."

Before the man knew what was happening, and before they had a chance to get up, Recker and Malloy sat down on opposite sides of him, surprising him.

"If you're thinking about using a gun, I'd strongly advise against it," Recker said with a smile.

"You don't look like a doctor," Malloy said. He put his hands inside the man's coat pockets and removed a gun, putting it inside his belt. Malloy then quickly patted the man down to see if he had anything else on him, which he didn't.

"What is this about?" the man asked. "I'm just a doctor having dinner with one of my nurses."

Malloy put his hand on the gun he just took off the man. "Oh yeah? This says otherwise."

"Just use it for protection."

"Really? This hospital in a bad neighborhood, is it?"

"I was about to go off shift, saw one of my nurses sitting here, decided to talk to her about something."

Malloy smiled. "You don't know who you're sitting with, do you?"

The man looked at Malloy, confused, knowing there was something he was missing. Malloy then pointed at Recker.

"See the guy on the other side of you?" Malloy leaned closer to him and whispered in his ear. "That's her boyfriend."

The man's shoulders slumped and hung his head, knowing that he was the one now in a jam.

"We know you don't work here."

"So how 'bout you tell us what you're doing here?" Recker asked.

"I'm not telling you guys nothin'."

"Now that is not the right attitude to have."

"Screw off."

"Sadko send you?"

The man looked at Recker and sighed, not even giving him the time of day. "C'mon, I'm not gonna tell you guys anything. If you wanna call the cops, then call them and let's go."

Malloy grinned. "Oh, you ain't getting off that easy. You know who I work for?" The man didn't seem to care. "I work for a man named Vincent." The man quickly spun his head to the side, obviously hearing the name before. "Oh yeah. That's right." Malloy leaned over again to whisper. "And I think he's gonna wanna talk to you."

"I'll still have nothing to say."

"I can be quite persuasive, you know."

"I'm not saying anything."

Malloy smiled, almost like he was going to enjoy the challenge. "We'll see." Malloy looked back at the doors and saw six of his men standing there, along with Haley. Malloy grabbed the man by the back of the shirt and pulled him off his chair and onto his feet. "C'mon, you're coming with us."

Before he was able to get more than a few steps away from the table, Recker grabbed Malloy's arm. "Wait a minute. Where are you taking him?"

Malloy motioned for his men to come forward, while he gave his prisoner a small push in the back to propel him onward. "Vincent's gonna want to talk to him."

"Where?"

Malloy shrugged. "I dunno. One of the usual spots, I guess."

"This is my deal."

"This is on everyone. They're after you now. But it's likely Sadko intends to make a run at Vincent too."

"And I know that. But I'm talking to him first."

"OK." Malloy motioned to his men to take the man out. "Take care of your girl and I'll see you out in the parking lot in a few minutes."

Recker thought he agreed to everything too easily, but then looked at Mia and didn't have time to worry about it.

"You OK?"

Mia sighed and nodded. "Yeah. Unfortunately I've had too much practice at this sort of thing."

"I know. I'm sorry."

"What was the story this time?"

"I don't know yet. I think he might work for the guy that took the shot at me."

"What was he gonna do with me?"

"I don't know."

"Well how did you know he'd be here?"

"Luck, really. Well, I guess it wasn't luck. Got a tip. Someone who knew Tyrell. The guy just happened to overhear their plans here."

"Well, that is kind of lucky. If he never heard, who knows what might have happened?"

"I dunno. I have a feeling you would have been protected, anyway."

"What, you mean Malloy?"

"There're more eyes here than I thought."

"Vincent put more men here?"

"Vincent's already got people here. Even before this?"

"What? He's got people working here all the time? How?"

Recker shrugged. "It's Vincent. That's really all that needs to be said."

"I guess so."

"I should be heading out. We'll still be leaving some people here so you don't have to worry."

"I'm fine."

"OK." Recker gave her a hug and a kiss, then found Haley by the doors and headed out of the hospital.

As Recker and Haley left the hospital entrance and walked through the parking lot, they heard tires squealing. Within seconds, they saw a few familiar vehicles zoom by. Malloy was in one of the cars. He rolled the window down and stuck his thumb out to give his friends a playful greeting as they drove away.

"Go after them?" Haley asked.

Recker took a deep breath and shook his head. "No, I doubt they're going to any of the usual places that we know. If they think we're just gonna show up anyway, I doubt they'd go through this."

"What's the point of ditching us?"

"I have a feeling Vincent's got something special in mind."

"Hope he clues us in."

"Somehow I doubt it."

9

Malloy, with the help of a couple of others, brought the man into a small ten by ten foot room. There was a wooden chair in the middle of the room, but nothing else except for the light fixture hanging overhead that didn't have a cover for it, exposing the dimly lit bulb. It was straight out of one of those old movie scenes where the cops are questioning the bad guys, using bad lighting to try to intimidate some key piece of information out of someone. Only this was no movie. There wasn't a single other thing in the room. Nothing on the walls, the floors were some kind of tile, though with the bad lighting, and the floor being dirty, it was hard to tell exactly what kind it was.

Malloy shoved the man onto the chair, then walked out of the room as the others held the man in place. He came back in less than a minute later, holding some zip ties in his hands. He walked behind the man and brought his hands in back of the chair and tied them together. The man immediately tried to free himself, but the ties were locked on tight, and he couldn't do so.

"What are you guys doing?!"

"You'll find out soon enough," Malloy said.

Then, he and the two others walked back out of the room, leaving the man alone for a few minutes to dream up some fears about what might be happening. Malloy and the others stood outside the door, waiting for Vincent to show up. He did five minutes later.

"What's the situation?" Vincent asked.

"Like I told you, we got him in the cafeteria, brought him right here," Malloy answered.

"Our friends?"

"Left them behind. Felt kind of bad ditching them like that, but..."

Vincent put his hand up. "I'll make it good with Mike. It had to be done this way. They most likely wouldn't approve of what we're about to do. We'll have more freedom to operate without them in the picture." Malloy nodded. "Ask him any questions yet?"

Malloy shrugged. "Asked him a few on the way over here. Didn't get anything. He's clamming up."

"Well we'll just have to do something about that, won't we? Jimmy in with me, you other guys stay out here."

Vincent walked into the room, Malloy right behind him, who then closed the door. The man in the hot seat was already sweating bullets. Ten minutes in a dark room with nothing but your own scary thoughts to keep you busy was enough for anyone to stomach.

"You know who I am?" Vincent asked. The man nodded. "Well that puts me at a disadvantage because I don't know who you are. Let's start with that."

The man looked at him, then Malloy, then figured he should get off on the right foot. "Jace."

Vincent grinned. "That's a good start. How about you now start by telling me what Sadko's intentions were with the girl at the hospital?"

Jace immediately started shaking his head. "I don't know. I don't know."

Malloy instantly stepped in and delivered a powerful right hand that rocked Jace's head back, almost tipping his chair over.

"You see, in interrogations such as this one, ambivalent answers are not the way to go," Vincent said. "I don't want to hear, I don't know. Or maybe. Or I'm not sure. Or anything else that signifies a weak response. You understand?"

Jace was squeezing his face to try to block out the pain from the right hand he just took. He spit on the floor to see if he was bleeding, which he wasn't. He was breathing heavier.

"What I want to hear is a legitimate and honest answer to my questions," Vincent said. "Is that understood?" Jace nodded. "So when I ask a question, you better give me the right answer. The honest answer. Any hesitations, any deceitful answers, anything that makes it look like you're trying to stall, you're gonna wind up in a lot of pain. I want to hear you say it."

"I understand."

"Good. Because I want to let another thought ruminate in that mind of yours. There's nobody coming for you. There's no one coming to save you. The only way you're leaving here on your own, is if I allow it. So if I don't feel as if you're helping me, you're going to leave here in a box. Nobody knows you're here."

"I understand."

"Good. What was Sadko planning on doing with the girl?"

Jace shook his head briefly. "I don't know. I really don't. He just said to get her and bring her to him."

"Where?"

"I don't know. He didn't tell me yet. He just said that when I had her, I was to call him, and then he would give me further instructions on where to go."

"Was he planning on killing her?"

"I don't know. I really don't know. He didn't say what his plans were."

"What are his plans overall?"

"I don't know."

Vincent sighed, already getting tired of hearing that answer. He looked at his underling and nodded. Malloy walked out of the room for a minute. While he waited, Vincent leaned his back up against the wall and looked at their prisoner. Malloy returned, holding a large pair of bolt cutters in his hand. Vincent detached himself from the wall and moved closer to the seated man.

"What are Justin Sadko's plans?"

"I don't know," Jace answered.

Malloy moved in behind the seat and knelt down, placing one of Jace's fingers in between the bolt cutters. He then started to squeeze them, causing an immense amount of pressure on Jace's finger. Jace closed his eyes and scrunched his face together and began tapping his foot on the floor to try to block out the pain.

"I'm not going to ask you again," Vincent said.

"I don't know! I don't know!"

Malloy immediately pressed down and twisted on Jace's index finger, about halfway to the knuckle, ripping part of the finger completely off the bone. Jace let out a terrifying scream as he felt the blood dripping from the part of his flesh where his finger used to be. Vincent looked on, unconcerned about the man's plight.

"You're going to need to get to a hospital soon," Vincent said calmly. "I would suggest working with us so you can get the help you need. Otherwise, we can keep you here for hours upon hours until a doctor is no longer needed. You'll bleed out, you'll go into shock, have an infection... I mean, I'm no doctor, so I can only assume that's what will happen. But I would think you don't have hours to wait. So I guess the question is now... how much do you value your life?"

Jace was in obvious pain from the expressions on

his face. He just wanted to keel over, though it wasn't possible with the ties holding him up to the chair. Malloy put his hand on his shoulder to also keep him in his current spot and not tip the chair over.

"Let's try this again," Vincent said. "Are you one of Sadko's men?"

"Yes."

"How many more does he have."

"I don't know," Jace said, breathing heavily.

Malloy took the bolt cutters and placed them on another finger. As soon as Jace felt them, he immediately started getting worried.

"How many digits would you like to lose?" Vincent asked.

"Umm, no, wait, I'll tell you, wait... uh, ten. No, fifteen. Yeah, fifteen."

Malloy took the cutters off his finger. Vincent continued his line of questioning.

"What are Sadko's plans?"

"Umm, he hasn't told me specifics."

"OK. Generalities."

"Uh, he wants to get The Silencer out of the picture."

"Why?"

Jace shook his head, still trying to catch his breath. "I don't know. He just feels that if he's gonna take over the city, he's gotta get rid of him first."

"So he has plans on taking me on as well?"

Jace nodded. "I think so. I think he first wanted to

get him out of the way. Then when he did, he was gonna try to start picking up territory from you."

"How was he going to accomplish that?"

"I don't know. He hasn't gone over specifics. He just says he knows how you operate and that he knows how he can start picking you apart a little at a time."

Vincent glanced at Malloy, slightly alarmed at the last statement. "Where is his base of operations?"

"He doesn't have a regular spot yet. That's one of the ways he said he can get over on you. If you don't know where he is all the time, then you can't mount a counter maneuver on him. He can always have the upper hand."

"He must have a spot where he gets everyone together."

"It changes every week."

"To where?"

"Different places. One week it's a motel room. The next week is in a park. Then a warehouse. Then an amusement park. Then a restaurant. It's never the same place twice."

"How does he communicate with everyone?"

"When he wants to meet, he gives everyone a couple hours of a heads-up, that way it doesn't leak out to anyone too far in advance."

"And other than that?"

"He just calls or texts people what he wants them to do."

"How is he recruiting people?"

"Umm, I don't know. He doesn't involve me in that."

"Well how did he recruit you?"

Jace looked around the room like he was having trouble focusing. "I don't know, he just found me one day."

"Where?"

"Umm, at a bar. Just came up to me and started talking. Seemed to know who I was already."

"How did he get you to get on board with him?"

"Uh, said there was a chance to make a lot of money. Said it wouldn't be easy and it might take some time. But we would have a lot of it if we could get a few people out of the way first. Asked if I was opposed to getting involved in some dangerous stuff or if I had a problem doing things that weren't legal."

"And of course you said you weren't."

"Hey, I got a record, we all know what kind of opportunities are out there for guys like me."

"I assume the rest of his staff is like you."

Jace shrugged. "I don't know. I guess."

"What else can you tell me?"

"Nothing, man. Can I please get to a doctor? My finger's killing me."

Vincent took a deep breath, considering his options, though he really felt he only had one. The man was never getting out of there alive, anyway. He wasn't going to just let Sadko have another of his men back so he could use it against him later. No, there was only one thing Vincent could do in his mind.

"I guess we're finished here," Vincent said.

Vincent then nodded at Malloy to do what had to be done. Malloy tossed the bolt cutters onto the ground, then removed his pistol. He pointed it at the back of Jace's head and instantly pulled the trigger. Jace's head slumped forward, though his restraints were keeping him upright and bound to the chair. Malloy put his pistol away and picked up the bolt cutters again to cut the zip ties. Once the restraints were gone, Jace slumped to the floor, falling face down.

Vincent stood over the lifeless man and looked at the back of his head. "No, it doesn't look like you're making it to a doctor today."

Malloy left the room to get the other two men, who came inside the room and dragged Jace's body away.

Once they were gone, Malloy wondered about their next steps.

"What do we do from here? Where do we go?"

"We keep digging," Vincent answered. "We keep digging until we strike gold."

10

Recker came walking through the door, getting a quick stare from his partners. After the incident at the hospital, Recker waited there until Mia was done work, then drove her to Haley's apartment, where they had been staying. Haley left to go back to the office. Jones was already aware of everything that went down.

"How is Mia?" Jones asked.

"She's fine," Recker answered. "She's tough. You know how she is."

"Yes, but, it still must be nerve-wracking for her."

"Have you heard from Vincent or Malloy yet?" Haley asked.

Recker shook his head. "No." He sighed. "Nope. Seems like they're avoiding me at the moment."

"Why do you think that is?" Jones asked.

"I don't know. They either want to get a leg up on me for some reason or..."

"Or what?"

"Or they're doing something they don't want me to know about or be involved in."

"What would that be?" Recker just looked at his partner, wondering if he really needed an answer to that softball of a question. Jones quickly realized his mistake. "Oh. Yeah. That."

Recker took a seat at the desk, though he didn't do anything initially. He just sat there, tapping his fingers down on the desk. One finger at a time. He kept staring at his fingers as they struck the desk, almost as if he were trying to keep them in rhythm as he played a tune with them. His partners could easily tell, though, that it was no tune that he was trying to play. Recker's look, his stare, his focus, it all told them one thing. Anger was seething out of him. It was just a question of who was going to get the brunt of it. It was a look they'd seen before, though not often. As was often the case, though, Jones couldn't help but inquire.

"At the risk of losing my head, to whom is your anger directed at the moment?" Recker leaned back in his chair as he continued tapping his fingers. "Is it the situation, Vincent, Malloy, something else?"

"Somebody out there is using her to get to me. Whether their plans were to kidnap her, or kill her, or god knows what else, they're using her as a target to get to me. And I don't like it."

"I completely understand."

"If someone wants me, then they should come after

me. They shouldn't bring in somebody who has nothing to do with anything."

"I get it."

"If they want to try and take me out, that's fine. Just tell me where and when and I will meet them wherever they want to. And then we can settle this and move on. They can bring whoever they want, whatever they want, and then we can end this. If they wanna do this like the wild west, fine, bring it on. Let's do it. But don't target innocent people who have nothing to do with it."

It was a lot of frustration talking, both Jones and Haley knew it, and they weren't going to try to talk him down at that point. They knew he just needed to blow off some steam. But they also knew there was another very real possibility. And that was that Mia wasn't out of danger.

"I hate to say this," Haley said. "But she's not out of the woods. They know where she works. That means they might try again. I'd even say it was likely."

"But it would be suicide at this point," Jones said, offering a contrary point of view. "By now they obviously know that she's being watched and protected there. That very well may prevent them from trying again."

"It won't. It'll just make them be more creative next time."

Recker sat there quietly, listening to his two partners debate the subject. He was letting things become more clear in his own mind. He was trying to let some of the anger fade away so he could think more clearly and rationally. After a few more minutes, he finally interjected himself into the conversation.

"It won't stop. If you try something once, the likelihood is that you're willing to try it again."

"Unless it fails miserably," Jones said. "In which case you move on to something else that you think may work."

"You're right. They probably won't try what they just did again. But it doesn't mean they won't try something else. If you want something bad enough, you'll keep trying things until you get it."

Recker picked up his phone and tried to call Malloy again. He still wasn't answering, though.

"What's our next move?" Haley asked.

"Well, it'd be nice if we knew what happened with the guy we just got at the hospital. If he sheds some light on stuff, we might have another direction to go in. Failing that, I guess it's just more of the same and waiting for another shoe to drop."

"Seems like we've been doing that a lot. Just waiting."

"Yeah, it does." Recker looked at Jones. "I guess you haven't pulled up anything else either?"

"No, but it might be helpful if we knew the identity of the man now in Vincent's possession. He didn't give you a name or anything?"

Recker put his hand on his forehead. "No, I don't think so. What about a picture?"

"What picture?"

"Can we go through pictures? Maybe I'll recognize him?"

"The problem there is... Sadko's group is so new that we don't know who he's associated with. The only thing we could do is look at pictures in police records, DMV files, things like that."

"That'll take years."

The trio each continued working, taking separate computers as they all began digging up different things that they hoped would develop into leads. Most of it centered on Sadko's background, hoping they could find the smallest nugget that they could turn to. Maybe an old girlfriend, a family member, anything that could give them an upper hand. After an hour of working, Recker's phone rang.

"Well look who it is," Recker said, seeing Vincent's name pop up on the screen. "Hello?"

"Mike. First off, I want to give my apologies for Jimmy taking off on you at the hospital and leaving you behind and in the dark. Those were on my instructions."

"I thought we were working together?"

"We are. But we all know we operate a little differently at times."

"I take it this was one of those?"

"It was. You may not have approved of our... methods."

"What methods were those?"

"It's neither here nor there."

"Where's the guy at now?"

"Honestly... he's at the bottom of a hole."

"Why?"

"Before you get huffy, we interrogated him first."

"And?"

"We got nothing. Sadko's being extremely careful at the moment. No base of operations, new meeting spot every week, doesn't tell people their assignments until a couple hours beforehand, he's being smart."

"From everything everyone's been telling me, this guy's got a screw loose. How can he be operating like this? Doesn't make sense."

"Perhaps I trained him too well."

"If he's as crazy as people think he is, he shouldn't be this hard to track down."

"What can I say? I agree. I don't know. Maybe he's had a transformation."

"Can you at least tell me the name of the guy that's no longer with us?"

"His name was Jace Hubbard."

"I'll start running him down and seeing if there's any connections."

"We've already started that process. No hits so far."

"No offense, but I'd put my money on our computer systems instead of yours."

"Fair enough. And again, I do apologize for the trickery."

"It's fine."

"And just so you know, I will keep my men there at the hospital to protect Mia for as long as it takes."

"Thank you. I appreciate that."

After hanging up, Recker tossed the phone down on the desk and sighed. The others could tell that the conversation did not go as well as any of them would have hoped.

"I take it that things did not go well," Jones said.

Recker took another deep breath. "You could say that."

"What about the guy they took?" Haley asked.

"Dead."

"What? How?"

Recker shrugged. "They probably beat out of him all the information that they could and then got rid of him when they were done."

"That's probably why they ducked out on us. Didn't want us to be involved in that."

Recker nodded. "Yeah."

"Did they get anything?" Jones asked.

"He said no. Except for a name. Jace Hubbard."

Jones immediately plugged the name into his database. Within a few seconds, they had everything they needed on him. His picture popped up, Jones turning toward Recker to make sure he was the one.

"That's him," Recker said.

Jace Hubbard was mostly a career criminal. He'd been arrested for robbery, assault, and kidnapping, though that wasn't all that he dabbled in. At first glance, it wasn't obvious as to how he would have known Sadko. They didn't appear to cross paths in prison, and Hubbard was never part of Vincent's crew. The connection wasn't clear. But there had to be one. Somewhere along the line, they must have crossed paths.

"Maybe it's not them themselves that knew each other," Recker said.

"How do you mean?" Jones asked.

"Well maybe they never did cross paths. Maybe one of them knew one of their sister's, or a friend, or a girl-friend, and that's how they got introduced."

"Possibly. I'll go through their backgrounds now to see if I can find something."

As Jones kept digging through their backgrounds, Recker sat there, staring at the screen. Something kept tugging at him. According to everyone that knew Sadko, though admittedly that was Vincent and Malloy, nothing suggested that he was the type of guy who could operate like this. And no matter what anyone thought of Vincent, he was an excellent judge of character in the men that he had, and the men he went up against. He had to be to survive as long as he had. He could read a man, or a situation, as well as anyone. And if men like Vincent and Malloy didn't believe someone like Sadko was capable of something like this, then the odds were that he wasn't. And that was the troubling part.

Haley glanced over at Recker several times. It was obvious there was something deeper on his friend's mind. More than just Sadko and Hubbard's background. There was something else.

"What else is bugging you?" Haley asked.

Recker snapped out of his daze and looked at his partner. He shook his head as he thought about it. "It's just... this doesn't seem right."

"Well it's not right."

"No, I mean... Sadko. Everything we've been told is he's unreliable, right?"

"Yeah."

"He's late, he's unstable, a little crazy, can't be counted on, all of that, right?"

"Yeah?"

"So Vincent said, according to Hubbard, that there's no specific meeting place. No base of operations, jobs aren't given out until a few hours before they have to do them, different spots for meetings, all of that... does that sound like the same guy to you?"

Haley shrugged. "Maybe he's learned some tricks."

"But this isn't a guy who worked for Vincent five years ago and has had time to learn and perfect things. This is a guy that was just with him a few months ago. That's not a long time to completely change who you are."

"So what are you saying?"

"I'm saying I find it hard to believe that he's the guy pulling the strings."

Jones stopped what he was typing and looked over at Recker. He then looked at Haley before putting his eyes back on Recker again.

"There's no evidence to suggest there is someone else involved," Jones said.

"Didn't say there was," Recker replied. "But I don't need evidence to believe something."

"You believe there's someone else in play here," Haley said. "Someone who pulled Sadko in."

Recker nodded. "I do. I just can't wrap my head around a guy like him calling all these shots and being able to avoid both me and Vincent. Doesn't seem like he's capable."

"Who could it be then?"

"I don't know. That's the question."

Jones put his hand up as he leaned his elbow on the desk, carefully measuring his words. "Just saying for a minute that you are correct and that Sadko is taking orders from someone else. What you are suggesting implies that it is someone from your past. Our past."

"Why?" Haley asked.

"Because if it was just someone who wanted to overtake the city, I believe the best method would have been trying to take out Vincent by surprise. They probably could have done that very effectively."

"Possible," Recker said.

"Since they did not, and targeted you first, that makes me believe it is someone with an axe to grind against you."

"Also possible."

"And the fact that they have targeted Mia indicates to me that it is somewhat personal."

Recker smiled. "Possible again."

"Who would that be?" Haley asked.

"If it's true, who knows? Could be anybody. I mean, we've literally dealt with hundreds of situations over the years."

"But who is capable of making it this personal?" Jones asked. "That is the question. A friend, a family member of someone we took care of, perhaps?"

Recker nodded while rubbing his lip. "Yep. Who is the question?"

11

After exhausting himself for most of the day, Jones finally slapped his hand down on the desk in frustration.

"Something wrong?" Recker asked.

"Yes, I'm done with this."

"With what?"

"Trying to find a connection between Hubbard and Sadko. There isn't one. It's just not there."

"That you can find."

"There isn't one. I've done an exhaustive search on this, trying to find the tiniest straws of hay, and there just is not one to be found. It doesn't exist."

Recker looked at him with a doubtful eye. "Really?"

"You're really going to doubt me?"

"I'm just saying... there has to be a connection somewhere. I mean, they didn't just look each other up on the bad guys anonymous group on some website. Right?"

Jones shrugged and threw his hands up. "I don't know. Perhaps they did. I cannot explain any other way they have found each other. I have dug into their backgrounds, their families backgrounds, friends, everyone they've known or come into contact with since they were fifteen years old. I have found nothing. No similar friends, no family members that know each other, they haven't crossed paths in prison, didn't go to similar schools, weren't born near each other, nothing. I've checked and rechecked and triple checked. There is no connection."

"You're sure?"

"A hundred percent sure. Well, maybe ninety-nine percent. And a half."

"If that's true," Haley said. "And I'm sure that it is, that gives more credence to the theory that someone else is pulling the strings here. That would explain why they don't know each other. Because they didn't put this together."

Recker nodded. "I agree. Question is how these guys were targeted to work for whoever hired them?"

"What about Mia?" Jones asked.

"What about her?"

"I take it she's being protected today?"

"Oh, she's not at work. She has the next three days off, so she's decorating."

"What?"

"My apartment," Haley replied. "She said it's a little lifeless. So she's... decorating."

"Oh," Jones said. "Well, at least that should keep her busy for a while."

"At least until we find a new place," Recker said.

"How is that coming along?"

Recker waved his hand in the air. "I dunno. She's mostly taking care of that. I've had too much on my mind to think about it. She's writing down a list of possibilities and then sometime next week we'll take a look at a few of them and figure out which one works for us best."

"So what's our next move here?" Haley asked. "Without a connection between Hubbard and Sadko, what do we do?"

Recker sighed, not having an answer. At least no good ones. "I don't know. I don't know if there's anything to do other than hope something breaks for us. Hubbard's dead, Sadko's in the wind, we don't know how they're involved, don't know where they are, don't know what they're planning, so we're pretty much operating in the dark with them."

"Hopefully Tyrell will come up with something."

"Or Vincent. I still get the feeling he might know more about what's going on than he's letting on. Or Hubbard told him more than he shared with us."

"Why?"

Recker shrugged. "Because it's Vincent. And he

always seems to know one more thing than everybody else."

"That's true."

"I dunno. Maybe we should just hit the streets and see if anything pops up. We don't have any jobs on the horizon, do we?"

Jones shook his head. "Not at the moment. I can always call you if something breaks."

"I feel like we got three days, with Mia being off and not having to worry about her, that we can really focus on just finding these jerks."

"Well, Tyrell's out there," Haley said.

A few minutes later, Recker's phone started ringing. "Ah, speak of the devil." Recker answered it. "What's up, Tyrell?"

"Yo, I just wanted to give you a heads up, I think I'm close to breaking this thing."

"What?"

"Yeah, I am close, man, real close."

Recker was actually a little stunned. "Uh, you're sure?"

"Positive. I got some bites out there that I'm just starting to reel in now."

"Well what's going on?"

"Can't say for sure, man, not yet. I don't got no specific names or anything. I just know that it's something big."

"Big like what?"

"Like I said, I don't have any names yet. I'm still working on that."

"Well you must have something you can tell me now."

"Just that there's someone in the past that you took out and someone's now gunning for you."

"I kind of figured that."

"Well that's all I got."

"Someone other than Sadko?"

"Please, man, that crazy boy couldn't be calling the shots on something like this. I hear he's just a stooge in all this."

"It's not Vincent, right?"

"What? Nah, man, that's just crazy. No, it's someone you killed or something a few years back. I ain't got the whole story yet. I'm waiting for one of my contacts now. He says he's got the whole story. Once I get it, I'll pass it along back to you."

"You trust this guy?"

"I mean, as much as I trust anyone in this business. You just hear what someone's got to say, consider their reputation, and then go from there. We'll see. What he told me so far makes sense. I'll see if the rest of it does."

"You want me to come down with you?"

"Nah, he'll only talk to me. Don't worry, I'll hit you up when it's over."

"All right. Let me know."

"Will do."

After Recker put his phone down, he just stared at

the desk for a moment. The others were waiting for an explanation.

"It sounded as if we might have a break?" Jones asked.

"Uh, yeah, maybe," Recker answered. He then retold everything that was said to him by Tyrell.

"Well that's good news," Haley said. "Maybe we'll be able to wrap this up soon and get back to normal."

"Maybe. Somehow I doubt it'll be that easy, though. It never is."

Tyrell was waiting at the back of the pool hall, just like he usually was when talking to this guy. He was one of Tyrell's regulars and often passed along useful tips to him when he had them. He'd never steered Tyrell wrong yet. While he was passing the time, Tyrell started playing a game of pool by himself. He looked at the time, noting that his guy was five minutes late. That should have been his first tip-off, since in the previous dozen or so encounters Tyrell had with him, he'd always been on time. But Tyrell figured everyone was late at one time or another. Must have been a heavy traffic night.

That five minutes quickly turned into thirty and now Tyrell was getting worried. Either what the man had was so big that he was afraid to share the information and was now blowing him off, or something had happened to him. Tyrell pulled out his phone and tried to call him. The number rang, but there was no answer. Tyrell tried three more times, getting the same result each time. He sighed, wondering how much more time he was going to give the guy. Since he was already there and waiting, he figured he'd wait another hour or so. He didn't have anything else that was pressing at the moment, so he could afford to wait. At least for a little while.

The pool hall was usually a bustling place and had a lot of activity, though on this night, there was something different about it. Tyrell had been there a bunch of times, but it never looked quite like this. Maybe it was the time of day, since he was usually there later, but the clientele looked different to him. It was a rougher-looking bunch than usual. And none of the people in there looked familiar. Every time Tyrell had ever been in the place, he recognized a few of the patrons as regulars. He looked at every table. There wasn't the same kind of life and exuberance as there usually was in the building. Something was off. He then looked at the person behind the counter, who he didn't recognize. He didn't think anything of it at first when he came in. He just figured it was someone new. But now that he was focusing on the rest of the people in there, it seemed weird.

Though he initially planned to wait another hour for his guy to show up, Tyrell was starting to get bad vibes as he looked around the room. He put the cue stick on the table and was about to head out. Just as he put it down, though, the front door opened up. Several men walked in, and then another man behind them walked in by himself. He was a bigger guy, well over six feet and two hundred pounds. He had a close-cut haircut and a thin beard. Tyrell knew the type. He knew this was bad news. The other men that were playing pool all suddenly stopped and looked at the man walking in. As Tyrell looked around the room, he knew he was alone. The man walked right up to Tyrell and shook his hand.

"Tyrell, good to see you again." Tyrell shook hands, trying to play it cool, though he knew something was going down. "If you're looking for the guy who was supposed to be meeting you here, well, it looks like he isn't able to make it." The man smiled as if he knew something nobody else did. "Looks like he had some kind of accident on the way over here. You shouldn't wait up for him."

"What'd you do to him?"

The man moved his head back like he was offended. "What'd I do? I didn't do nothin'. I told you, traffic's a bitch out there today. It's not fit for man nor beast. Accidents are happening all over the place."

There was an unmistakable worried look on Tyrell's face. He knew he had to watch what he said and did closely and not make any sudden moves or say anything stupid.

You probably don't remember me, do you? I was a member of..."

"I remember you," Tyrell said. "I know who you are."

"Well that's good. Gives us a good first step."

"In what?"

"I want Mike Recker, man. I want The Silencer."

Tyrell shrugged. "So what are you doing here, then?"

"You're one of his boys, aren't you?"

"Nah. We're not that tight."

The man started laughing. "Now that's funny. You see, it's all over this city. Everyone I talk to says the same thing. That you're in tight with him."

"It's not like that. I've done a few jobs for him here and there, just like I did for Vincent, Jeremiah, the Italians, and anybody else who's got the money. But we ain't like buddy-buddy or anything."

"Now you're just messing with me. You and me both know you never did any jobs for the Italians. I was around then."

"So what are you doing back here, man?"

"Reclaiming what was going to be rightfully mine at some point before your boy took it away."

"He's not my boy."

"Yeah, well, at this very minute, you better hope he is."

"Why's that?"

"Because your life might depend on it."

"He ain't gonna make no deals for me," Tyrell said.

The man nodded, though he didn't believe that for a second. "We'll see."

"What are you gonna do?"

"Just want to have a chat with him, man. That's it. And you're gonna make that happen."

"I don't have his number."

"You expect me to buy that?"

"It's true. Anytime he wants me, he calls me from different numbers. Burner phones. Never the same one twice. He's careful like that. Even if I had his number, it wouldn't do any good. He'd already have switched to three new phones in that time."

"Well then you'll use your contacts with Vincent to make it happen."

"Vincent ain't gonna do that."

"Well then you're a dead man. You either find a way to get a message to Recker or else I'm just gonna put a bullet in your head now. Which will it be?"

Tyrell sighed and looked around the room. He'd run out of choices.

As Recker waited for news from Tyrell, he paced around the room, as he often did. Jones sighed as he passed him a few times. The pacing drove him crazy, and sometimes was distracting for him, though he knew it often calmed Recker down.

"Will you just sit down and work on something?" Jones said.

"How can I work on something when I know Tyrell might have the answer to this whole thing now?"

"He'll call when he has something."

"I didn't even get a time. I should've asked what time he was meeting this guy."

"Or woman."

"Whatever. You know what I meant."

"You said he was waiting for someone to contact him. There might not have been a specific time. Maybe he's still waiting."

"Why don't you try calling him again and see what's up?" Haley asked.

"Tried a few minutes ago," Recker said. "Went to voicemail. Whenever his phone goes straight to voicemail, that usually means he's tied up with something."

"Well then just wait for him to call," Jones said.

"That's what I'm doing." Recker continued walking around the room.

"I meant by doing something else."

"This calms me."

"You don't say?"

When Recker's phone started ringing on the desk, he stopped his pacing and dashed for it. He was slightly disappointed to see that it wasn't Tyrell. But maybe Malloy had something useful for him.

"Hope this is short," Recker said. "I'm kinda in the middle of something."

"Does what you're in the middle of involve Tyrell?"

"How do you know?"

"Just got a message from him."

"What? Why would you get a message from him?"

"I don't know. Apparently he's in some kind of trouble."

"What kind of trouble?"

"I don't know."

"What's the message?"

"It came into one of my guys, who passed it along to me. Looks like he's been taken."

"Taken? By who?"

"Message doesn't say," Malloy answered. "Just says to give this message to you. Says if you want Tyrell back unharmed, to come to the Doublemint Hotel, room 648, alone."

"What time?"

"Tonight. Eleven PM."

"Who sent it?"

"Apparently it came from Tyrell's phone, so whoever grabbed him must have known his connections. What's going on? What was he doing?"

"Working on the Sadko thing. Said he was close to figuring out who was behind it all. Was supposed to be meeting with someone and then he'd know."

"Well, I'd say he found out now."

"The message say anything else?"

"Just says to come alone, no tricks on either side."

"Sounds like they just wanna talk."

"If you believe them at their word."

"Not sure if I have a choice."

"There's always a choice."

"There isn't when someone's life is at stake."

"Sure there is," Malloy said. "Just depends on how much you value it."

"There's no choice to make on this one."

"Well, if you need me on this one, you know where to find me."

"Thanks." Recker put the phone down and looked at his partners. "We got a problem."

12

After explaining the situation to the others, Recker looked at the time.

"Looks like we got two hours until then."

"What's the play?" Haley asked.

Recker shrugged, not having an answer except for the obvious one. "I go in there at eleven o'clock and get him out."

Jones took off his glasses and rubbed his eyes. "That's not a plan."

"It's the only one I got. And we don't exactly have a lot of time to create one."

"As terrible as this is to suggest, and I know you will push back on it, but there is also one major consideration that we have to think of."

"I probably know what you're gonna say, but say it anyway."

"We don't know for sure whether Tyrell is even

alive."

Recker shook his head. "Don't matter."

"I knew that would be your reaction, but it is something that we still need to consider."

"You consider it. Doesn't change anything from my perspective. I'm assuming he's there. And I'm getting him out. That's the only thing I'm considering."

"I'm not saying we shouldn't do anything. I'm just saying it needs to be thought of."

"Doesn't sound to me like there's gonna be any tricks," Haley said. "Sounds to me like someone who wants a conversation and doesn't know any other way to go about it."

"Could be," Recker said. "But if they just wanted a conversation, why go after Mia?"

"Maybe after the failure of that they decided to change course?"

"Does who this might possibly be change anything?" Jones asked.

"It doesn't," Recker replied. "Doesn't matter who it is at this point. Looks as if we're about to find out soon enough, anyway."

"No, but it might have been helpful to figure out who it was and have some inkling of what or who you might be going in there with. At least it would have helped to prepare."

"The only thing I need help preparing for now is figuring out how I'm getting in and out without getting killed."

"Besides the obvious fact of not going?"

"Yeah."

Haley was wracking his brain on it. "I mean, I can keep a watch on you throughout the hotel, in the lobby, the hallway, all of that, but once you're in that room, outside of me getting in there and hiding somewhere, I'm not sure how I can cover you."

"Let's pull up photos of the hotel."

"Already on it," Jones said.

They started going through pictures of the perimeter of the hotel, aerial photos, pictures of the inside, everything they could get their hands on. There were no obvious spots for Haley to set up in.

"Can you pull up which side of the building that room number is on?" Recker asked.

"Should be able to," Jones replied. He kept typing for another minute, bringing up several pictures, which disappeared from the screen shortly afterwards. Finally, he brought up another picture that he kept on the screen. "This is it. It's on the west side of the building."

"OK, what's on that side?"

Jones brought up some more pictures, all of them focusing on the outside of the building.

"Wait a minute," Haley said. "Go back."

Jones clicked to go back a couple of pictures. It was of the building across the street from the hotel. They all stared at the picture for several seconds.

"Yeah, I think that's gonna be my best bet."

Jones turned his head, though he still kept his eyes on the screen, thinking he was missing something. "What exactly are you seeing that I am not?"

"That hotel is six floors, right?"

"Yes."

"Building across from it is about the same height. I can cover through the window."

"You might not even be able to get a look from there."

"I'll have to make it work."

"What is that building, anyway?" Recker asked.

Jones typed away for a minute or two until he got the answer. "Looks like some kind of office building."

"Should be perfect," Haley said. "About the same height. At night. Nobody will be in there. I should be able to pick my spot."

"But that still doesn't mean you will get a good view of Michael through that window."

"No, but I can try. As far as I can see it's the best option we got."

Recker nodded., seeing the same thing as his partner. "I agree."

"Will you be able to get into that building?" Jones asked.

"I've broken into some of the toughest places imaginable over the years," Haley said. "I think I'll be able to manage an office building."

"I'll have to try and make it over to a window once I'm inside that room so you can get yourself a target."

"What if you're never able to make it there?" Jones asked.

"I'll do what I can."

"I guess the second part of my question there is, what if they decide to kill you on the way to the room, or as soon as you step foot into that room? Tyrell could be dead already for all we know. This might just be a ploy to get you there alone and do you in as well."

"We'll just have to take that chance."

Jones took a deep breath, not liking that answer. He liked having a more definitive answer behind any moves they made. He hated leaving things to chance and guesswork. But it was what it was at that point.

"Hey, can you hack into the hotel database and see who's staying in that room?" Recker asked.

Jones immediately started typing. "Shouldn't be too hard." After a few more minutes, he had an answer, though his face indicated it wouldn't be pleasing to anyone.

"What?"

"The room is registered to a Randall Moore."

"Generic name. Could be anybody. Oh well. Guess we'll find out when I get there."

Before they started to get themselves ready, Recker picked up his phone again so he could tell Mia he wouldn't be home for a while.

"Who are you calling?" Jones asked.

"Mia. Want to let her know what's going on so she doesn't worry."

"What are you going to tell her?"

"What's happening."

"And you think that's going to make her not worry."

"There was a time when I tried to hide what I was really doing from her," Recker said. "It was you, I believe, and her, who said that wasn't a good idea."

"Yes, well, within reason. Telling her you're marching into a hotel with unknown bad guys not knowing if you're going to make it out wasn't exactly the kind of truth serum I had in mind when I said that."

"I'm not keeping secrets from her anymore. She's too smart for that, anyway."

"It's your funeral. Hopefully not literally. Before you do that, though, should we call Malloy back to see if he can provide assistance?"

Recker raised his eyebrows at him. "You actually want to call him for assistance? That's an unusual departure for you. Usually you do everything possible to avoid dealing with them."

"As I have done a few times in the past, I will contact them when it is necessary. I don't believe in asking them for help when it is not crucial. But in this case..."

Recker shrugged. "What's he gonna do that we're not? Have a second guy in the window next to Chris?"

"Maybe he can set up in the hotel somewhere?"

"What for? If they're gonna try and kill me they'll do it inside that room. He wouldn't get to me in time.

And there might be people outside the door, anyway."

Jones shook his head. "I don't like this."

"Who does? It's the situation we're dealing with. Gotta play the cards you're dealt."

"It would be nicer if we had an ace up our sleeve though."

Recker called Mia, who picked up on the second ring. Him calling so late at night usually only meant one thing. Something came up, and he wasn't making it home before she went to bed. Upon answering, she didn't even give him time to explain.

"Uhh, let me guess. Something came up and you might be a while and you don't know when you'll be home? Am I in the ballpark?"

"You're at home plate."

Mia sighed, but understood. "What's going on?"

Recker hesitated before answering, but wasn't going to lie about it. "Someone took Tyrell."

"What do you mean someone took him? Took him where?"

"They're holding him and wanna talk to me. That's apparently the only way they'll let him go."

"Does this have to do with our situation?"

"I think so."

"You have to get him," Mia said. "You can't just leave him there."

"I'm not. We're working out a plan now."

"Is it a trap?"

Recker sighed. "I'm not sure. It might be. And maybe they really do just want to talk."

"Is Chris going?"

"Yeah."

"I know you'll be as safe as you can."

"You keep the bed warm for me, OK? I promise you I'll be there with you in a few hours."

"Just be careful, OK?"

"You know there's nothing that will stop me from coming home to you."

"I know. I love you."

"I love you more."

Recker put his phone down and looked at Haley, giving him a nod that he was ready to go.

"Let's lock and load."

The two of them got all of their weapons ready and headed out of the office. They took separate cars, just in case there was going to be any fireworks after, that way they had more opportunities to split if things spilled over into the street. By the time they got near the hotel, there was a little under an hour left until the meeting time. They split up, with Haley going over to the office building to break his way in, while Recker stayed on the outside of the hotel, closely watching the entrance. A few minutes later, he heard from Haley.

"I'm in. Making my way up to the fifth floor."

"Let me know when you're in position," Recker said.

Recker kept his eyes peeled out front, hoping that

eventually he would see Tyrell, or some of the people who had taken him, go through the front doors. At least that way he would see that his friend was still alive, as well as how many people he was dealing with. He wasn't even as concerned about who it was at the moment. He was more worried about getting Tyrell back, and the both of them making it out alive. The identity of who had taken him was secondary at this point.

Once the hour was up, Recker was a little concerned that he hadn't seen anyone up until then. A few people came in and out of the hotel, but it didn't look like anyone that he was looking for.

"Looks like I'm heading in."

"See anything yet?" Haley asked.

"Negative. It's time to go in, though. How's your position?"

"It's good. As of right now, though, I'm not sure how much help I can be. I can't tell the specific room you'll be in and a bunch of them have the curtains closed so I can't see inside, anyway."

"Once I get in there, I'll have to find a way to look out the window so you can see me."

Now raining, Recker walked across the street and made his way inside the lobby of the hotel. Almost immediately, he was met by someone. It wasn't quite what Recker had expected. He thought he was going to be able to just go up to the room by himself. Now it looked like he was going to have an escort.

"I take it you're the man?" a larger man asked.

"Depends who's asking," Recker replied.

The man smiled. "Yeah, you're the man. We're here to take you up there."

"OK. So take me."

"First, we gotta frisk you and make sure you're not packing."

Recker took a step back. "Well that's gonna be a problem right there. Ain't nobody frisking me, especially not you, and I'll tell you right now I'm packing."

The man shook his head. "Boss said no guns."

"Boss can kiss my ass. I'm not heading into anything I don't know unprotected."

"He said no guns or you don't get your friend."

Recker shrugged, thinking they were bluffing. "Then I guess it's no deal. I'm not going anywhere unarmed."

The man looked at Recker for a few seconds, then another of the guards. "Wait here." The man took out his phone and walked away while the other guard stayed with Recker. The conversation on the phone only took about thirty seconds. He walked back over. "Boss said you can keep your guns."

Recker grinned. "Kind of him."

The man nodded for him to follow him as he started walking. "This way."

They walked to the elevator and got in. Another guest tried to get into it as well, but was shooed away by one of the guards. Not a word was said by any of them as the elevator lifted off the ground and made its way up. Upon reaching the fifth floor, the three men got out and walked over to the room. It was obvious which one it was as there was a man standing on the outside of it keeping guard. They walked over to the room, the guard at the door opening it and letting the three men inside. As soon as he stepped inside the room, Recker looked around, surprised that no one else was in there.

"What's going on?" Recker asked.

"Boss will be with you in a minute. He likes to make a grand entrance."

"Nice."

Recker started walking over to the window, taking note of where the window was in position to the couch and chair that was set up. His movements made the guards antsy.

"What are you doing?"

"I've got some bad feelings about this." Recker made his way to the window and opened the curtain a little. "Looking out windows helps to calm me down."

"Kinda weird a little."

"The alternative is that I kill the both of you before your boss gets here. That always makes me calm."

"Sure of yourself, aren't ya?"

"Yep."

"I'm kind of hoping you'll get your chance to prove it."

Recker looked at him and smiled. "Me too."

13

Recker was sitting in the chair, wondering what it was all about, when he saw several people walking through the door. It was apparent they were the bodyguards for someone. They just had that look and feel to them. Recker was calm, though curious, as he waited for whoever the main guy was. A few of the guards came into the room, with Tyrell in the middle of them. At least Recker now knew that he was alive. Tyrell was taken to the side of the room. Recker looked at the way his friend walked, his face, studying him to make sure he wasn't limping or had any marks on him to suggest he'd been beaten. There was nothing obvious to suggest that he was. After the guards stepped to the side of the door, another man came through it. The way everyone looked to him, it was obvious he was the guy Recker was waiting for. He was the guy in charge.

As the man walked to the table, Recker studied

his face. He tried to remember when or where he might have bumped into him before. He couldn't place him, though. There was something familiar about him, but Recker was fairly sure he'd never seen the guy before. Recker had an outstanding memory, and could remember faces he only saw in passing from ten years ago in his CIA days from a mission in China. But even though there was something familiar about this man, Recker was sure he'd never come across him before.

The man finally came to the main part of the room and sat down across from Recker. The two stared at each other, the way two boxers do just before a match, each trying to intimidate the other before the battle begins. The man looked over at one of his men and motioned to him.

"Set us up with something," the leader said.

Recker and his host continued staring at each other as they waited for their drinks to arrive. A minute later, a man came over, a rum and coke for each of them, and set them down on a small table in front of them. The leader of the group took a sip of his, though Recker didn't touch his at all.

"You gonna drink that?"

"I don't usually drink until I know what I'm drinking for," Recker replied.

"To our relationship."

In his mind, Recker was instantly trying to place the voice somewhere. Again, it was something familiar, though the exact tone didn't strike him as something he knew. "Didn't think we had one."

"Well we do."

Recker grinned. "News to me."

The man looked around the room. "Nice place here, don't you think? One of the better hotels I've been in."

"I guess it's fair."

"I guess you're curious about who I am, what you're doing here, all that, right?"

"It crossed my mind."

"You don't know me, do you?"

Recker shook his head. "No. Should I?"

"You've seen me before."

"I have?"

The man nodded. "It was a few years back. And you weren't dealing with me directly. But I was there."

"Don't remember you."

"My name's Jerrick."

"Jerrick. That a first name or last name?"

"Either."

"Oh, so it's Jerrick Jerrick. Nice."

"You always so cute?"

"I try. Sometimes I even use a teddy bear as a prop."

Jerrick laughed. "Funny man."

Recker shrugged, amused with himself.

"I used to have a cousin named Jeremiah." Recker's eyes immediately lit up upon hearing the name. Now he knew exactly what this was all about. "I say used to... because he's dead now. But you obviously know that, don't you? Because you're the one that killed him."

"As far as I know he was killed in a police raid."

Jerrick snickered. "Yeah, that's what everyone's supposed to believe, isn't it?" Jerrick picked up his drink and almost pointed it at his guest. "But you and I know different, don't we?"

Recker shrugged. "Does it matter? I'm not really interested in living in the past. You shouldn't either."

"Oh, but it does matter. It does matter. You know why? Because Jeremiah was family. He was like a brother to me."

"Then you would know that Jeremiah did some things that he shouldn't have and paid the price for it. End of story. Time to move on."

"That's not how it works, man. Not in this game."

"It's exactly how it works. For anybody who plays it. You screw up, you get banged. It's as simple as that. If Jeremiah had played his cards on the straight and narrow, he might still be alive and breathing today. But he didn't. He went for a big score and got burned. That was his mistake. And he paid the price for it."

"Maybe so. Doesn't change what I'm doing here though."

"Which is what exactly? Getting payback on me?"

Jerrick shrugged. "Maybe. See, I was in Jeremiah's crew right before all that nonsense with you went down." He could see in the look of Recker's eyes that he didn't quite believe him. "Yeah, that's right. I was there. You see, I was in the room a couple of those times that you met with Jeremiah. Maybe you didn't notice me much because I wasn't a big man then. I was just standing guard, things like that. Probably not big enough to catch your attention."

"So?"

"So a few weeks before Jeremiah got killed, he sent me and three other guys away. Wanted us to learn the business, so to speak. We would eventually be his succession plan. We'd take over after he was done."

"So he sent you away to do it?"

"He wanted us to start carving out our own territory somewhere else. Start making our own path with the skills and the knowledge that he taught us. Then when we were ready to take over for him, it'd be a smooth transition. We could move right in without missing a beat."

Though it was a nice story, Recker didn't seem all that motivated by it. He honestly really didn't care about his backstory. All that mattered to him was the present and how it affected him.

"So for the last two years, that's what we've been doing. Making our own path."

Recker faked a smile. "I'm proud of you."

Jerrick leaned forward. "You know, as a man of your stature and reputation, you should probably show more respect to someone who literally holds your life in their hands right now. Look around, there's ten of us here. If I say the word, you're a dead man right now."

"You think so?"

"Yeah, I do. What, you gonna tell me you got a bomb under the table or something?"

"Nope. But if you think I'm here by myself than you're more stupid than you look."

Jerrick sat up straight again, and his eyes flickered around the room for a few seconds. "Oh, I forgot. There's that other Silencer running around these days, isn't there? That's new from when I was here last. How many more you got? Two, three?"

"It'll feel like a hundred to you by the time I'm done with you."

"Yeah, Jeremiah only had to deal with you, didn't he?"

"What exactly is your play here?" Recker asked. "Revenge on me for killing Jeremiah?"

"I got a lot of goals, man. A lot of goals. And I aim to accomplish all of them. Number one, I'm gonna kill you. Not here. Now now. But I'm gonna kill you. You took my cousin away. That don't fly with me. It don't fly at all. Number two, before I kill you, I wanna take away all that you have. That means that girlfriend of yours. I want you to experience loss and heartbreak."

"Listen, stupid, I've experienced more loss, hardship, and heartbreak in the last ten years than you'll ever experience in a hundred. If you think killing my girlfriend is somehow going to crush me and make me

143

feel something I've never felt before than you're an even bigger moron than you seem to be."

"Maybe so. But even more than that, I want you to pay in every way for what you did."

Recker shook his head and sighed. "You're as stupid as he was. And you'll likely suffer the same fate as him, too. Him and I were fine until he stepped over the line. You should learn from his mistakes. Because they'll be your mistakes, too."

"And even beyond you, I want to pick up what he started. He wanted complete control over this city. He already had part of it. Then when you did what you did, Vincent was easily able to take control of the rest of it. Now he's got it all. Well guess what? I'm taking it back."

"So why has it taken you two years to come back for this grand plan of yours?"

"Because if I did it right then and there... I wasn't ready. I wasn't ready then to take on a man like you. Or Vincent. I didn't know what I was doing. I didn't know how to lead my own crew yet. I didn't know how to make the tough decisions. I didn't know how to lay low, pick apart my enemy from a distance."

"But now you do?"

"But now I do. You see, I've been here for the last five months. And neither you or Vincent knew about it. I've just been building my organization one brick at a time. One brick at a time."

"Well if you've been here five months and didn't

take out Vincent by surprise when you had the chance, I really doubt you're gonna accomplish that now."

Jerrick smiled. "Listen, do I look worried?"

"No, you don't. Maybe because you're too stupid to know better."

"You call me stupid one more time and we're gonna have a problem right here and now."

Recker stared at him for a few seconds. "Stupid."

They continued staring at each other for a little while. Then Jerrick finally broke the tension with a small laugh. "You're trying to provoke me. I get it. I get it. Ain't gonna work."

"You know, I really don't know what you hoped to accomplish with all this. You tried to take me out by surprise... didn't work. You tried to take Mia, didn't work. You've now blown your cover by revealing yourself to Vincent so you can't even take out his crew by surprise either. I really don't understand what you're doing here. It really makes no sense."

"I'm not afraid of you. I'm not afraid of Vincent. There's where most people who come up against either of you fail. They're afraid. They have to operate in secrecy because they feel that's the only way they can win. Well I'm not like that. These last few months I've been here strictly to build up my organization. To get us up to the numbers we need to be. Then we can start taking back what's rightfully ours. What Jeremiah began to build. I'm gonna finish it for him."

"You'll get buried right next to him."

"You want a war, Vincent wants a war, we'll give it to you both. I'm not here to play games. We're here to win."

Recker sighed, knowing the conversation was only going to continue to go one way. "Listen, you wanna wage war on me, fine. You wanna take out Vincent, that's his business. Fine. I can handle that. You won't be the first to take me on and lose, and you won't be the last either. But leave it at that. Don't be targeting innocent people that have nothing to do with it."

Jerrick grinned. "Ahh, you mean the pretty nurse, don't you? What's the matter, afraid you can't protect her? The big bad Silencer can protect everyone in the city but can't protect his own girlfriend?"

"I'm just telling you... lay off."

"And I'm just telling you... everything's on the table. I ain't got no standards that I won't cross, lines I won't go over. Everything's fair game in this business."

"I guess we've said everything we've got to say then." Recker slowly stood up.

"Yeah. I guess we have. We'll be seeing more of each other. But then again, maybe we won't."

Recker looked at Tyrell and motioned for him to come over. "C'mon, Tyrell, we're leaving."

Tyrell walked over to him and stood behind him.

Jerrick pointed at him. "You're on borrowed time too. When he goes, you're going with him."

"We'll see about that," Tyrell said.

"Yes, we will. You've been at this a long time,

playing multiple sides of the fence. You're with him, with Vincent, Jeremiah, and every other person that's come in here. Well not no more. You're probably one of the reasons people like him and Vincent got to where they are. You'll snitch on anybody for a dollar."

Tyrell shook his head. "That's not true. I'd snitch on you for nothin'."

"I think we're done here," Recker said. "First one of you that goes through that door after us is gonna get your head blown off."

Jerrick smiled, not looking worried. "You ain't gotta worry about that today. Today's your hall pass. Today you got a freebie. Tomorrow, though... tomorrow's a different story. Tomorrow we're coming gunning for you."

"You better come with both barrels then. Because I'm gonna have a double barrel pointing straight at you."

"I guess we'll see which one of us comes out standing."

"Yeah. I guess we will."

14

After leaving the hotel, Recker took Tyrell back to his house. Haley followed them just to make sure they didn't run into trouble. Recker and Tyrell stood just outside his house as they discussed the situation.

"You're gonna have to be really careful from now on," Recker said. "They know who you are, where to find you, and what you're doing."

"Don't worry about me. I'll do what I always do."

"Just watch yourself."

Tyrell nodded. "Thanks for coming for me."

"Wasn't even a question."

"What do you think that was about?"

"Huh?"

"Back there. I mean, why go through all that? Why expose himself like that? He didn't have to. He could've continued operating in the shadows. Or he could've killed the both of us in that hotel. Why let us go if he's planning on killing us, anyway."

"I was thinking about that on the drive over here," Recker said. "I think he feels it's just the next logical progression. Operating in the shadows has worked to a point. Then when he tried to do take me out, and take Mia out, they both failed. Now he's got no other options. He knows we're watching at the hospital, so the surprise factor is gone. He has no idea where I am, so that's not an option either. In order to keep a target on us, he's gotta go public, knowing that we're gonna be out there looking for him too. I guess he figures at some point we're going to expose ourselves. And he hopes to capitalize on it when we do."

"I guess I can understand that. But why all that jazz with taking me to the hotel? He could've finished us."

"I think he knew if anything started, I was taking him out as well. I didn't let them take my guns before I went in, so he knew I was armed. If there was any funny business, he was only a few feet away from me. He'd be the first one I killed if someone did something stupid."

"Yeah, I guess that explains it too." Tyrell shook his head, trying to understand everything that had been going on. "Just a lot to process right now."

"Yeah, it is."

"How'd they find you when they took that shot at you on the street?"

"I dunno. My guess is that they had followed Mia to

the apartment and then followed us downtown. Then they saw us walking and took their shot."

"Yeah, but who was the target? You or her?"

Recker looked away and shook his head. "I don't know. It honestly could've been either of us. I assumed it was me, but hearing what he said about wanting me to feel loss, it could've been her too."

"Seems like we got a big security problem now. He knows where your girl works. He knows where I live. He's got access to you."

Recker sighed and rubbed his forehead. "Yeah, we're gonna have to see what we can do to change that."

"We might not see them, but you can bet your ass they're gonna be watching. Me and her."

"I know."

"And they're gonna hope one of us screws up and leads them back to you."

"We're just gonna have to be extra careful. Might be good if me and you don't meet for a while. At least until this simmers down a little to where we can be sure there's nobody watching."

"Yeah, I agree. What's the deal with Sadko then? Jerrick just using him for, what?"

"I assume he wanted someone who was familiar with the inside of Vincent's organization. Someone who could provide him with some answers. He needed someone to get a glimpse of how Vincent operates, what he does, how he thinks. That's something that Jeremiah never had."

"I still think he blew his chance here, man. He could've really opened up a big one on Vincent by catching him by surprise. He should've taken it."

"I think he really just wanted to take me out first. Maybe with Sadko, he figures he's got an inside line on Vincent anyway that he can use anytime."

"Yeah, maybe."

Recker continued thinking, a new thought playing in his head over and over again. And it was one he couldn't shake. "Unless..."

"Unless what?"

"Unless it wasn't a surprise."

"What do you mean?"

"Maybe the reason he wasn't trying to take Vincent by surprise was because he knew he couldn't."

"Why couldn't he?"

"It's not a surprise if your opponent already knows you're coming."

Tyrell raised his eyebrows. "You think Vincent already knows about all this?"

Recker shrugged. "I don't know. I'm just throwing things out there. But now that I'm thinking about it more clearly, maybe it makes sense. Now that I'm thinking about it, at no time has Vincent seemed that upset about one of his men up and leaving his organization. He's kind of taken it in stride."

"If one of his men left, he'd want to know why. He'd

want to know where they were going, and what their plans were after they left."

"Yeah. He wouldn't just let them go and give them a fruit basket as a parting gift. He'd want to know and make sure they weren't coming back to bite him later on."

"So maybe he has known this entire time," Tyrell said.

"I think it's possible."

As they continued talking, Recker's eyes glanced down the street at a parked car. He was careful not to keep his head looking directly at it. Instead, he turned his head back to Tyrell, while still keeping the car in the corner of his vision to look at it.

"What?" Tyrell asked, noticing Recker's distraction.

"Just act cool like nothing's wrong."

"Is there?"

"Not sure. There's a green sedan parked down the street."

"So? There's cars here every day."

"This one's got two men inside."

"So? They might live there, you know. Maybe they're smoking a joint. Maybe they're just talking. Maybe they're waiting for a lady friend to do a little back seat party?"

"Maybe. I just wanna make sure that we're not being watched now. We could've been followed here. Or maybe they were already waiting here for when you got back."

Tyrell was now coming around to his friend's way of thinking. "Uh, I don't know how to tell you this, but I think you might be right on that car."

"Why?"

"Because I think I spot another one down there."

Recker was careful not to turn around and look and give it away that they were on to them. "What's it look like?"

"Uh, blue four-door, two men inside. One of them just lit a cigarette."

Recker casually touched his earpiece. "Chris, you hearing this?"

"I'm on it," Haley replied.

A few seconds later, they noticed Haley's car driving down the street. He was driving slow, though still not making it obvious he was trying to check out the occupants of both cars. Once he drove off the street, he reported back with his findings.

"Mike, looks like the problem's confirmed."

"How so?"

"Saw a gun in both cars."

"You sure?"

"In the first one, there was a gun on the lap of the driver. Just sitting there."

"And the other?"

"Looked like the passenger had it in his hand. He tried to duck it down to the side of him as I drove by to conceal it."

"Maybe they're cops," Tyrell said.

"Since when did cops stake you out?" Recker asked.

"First time for everything."

"So what do you wanna do?"

"Me? What do you want me to do?"

"Well it's your house. Your neighborhood. Your street. I figured you should get some say about what goes on."

"I ain't killing all them dudes."

"I didn't say you did. I just asked what you wanna do."

"Well what are the options?"

"One, we kill them."

"Didn't I just say that?"

"Or, we leave them alone. Let them stay and watch."

"And hope I mess up."

"Well there's a good countermeasure to that."

"Yeah? What is it?"

Recker smiled. "Don't mess up."

"Gee, thanks."

"You know, even the best ones stumble from time to time."

"So you're saying you're in favor of taking them out then?"

"That's not what I'm saying. What if you kill these dudes and Jerrick thinks it was me?"

"He won't."

"What if he does?"

"He won't."

"How do you know?"

"Because he won't. He'll know it was me. That's just a given."

"What if this brings down more heat on me?"

"Shouldn't."

"What makes you so sure?"

"Because dead bodies usually increase the police presence in that area for the few days and weeks after that. Might actually help you get loose a little."

"That's only temporary."

Recker shrugged. "Only other thing you can do is move."

"What good will that do? If Jerrick's been here for five months, he's probably already started putting men out all over the place. Some of them might even be hanging out in places I tend to visit. He knew I was at that pool hall when he took me. Even if I move, he might still know where I am."

"Possible."

"You're not giving me a lot of options here."

"Sure I am. Just no good ones."

"Well, what do you think?"

"I say take them out. Jerrick's a threat. Anytime you can take out four men of that threat and whittle their forces down, that's a win in my book. You take them whenever you can get it."

"You were planning on doing that all along, weren't you? Regardless of what I said."

"Yeah. Because it's also possible they're just here to

try and kill me. If they thought the hotel was too risky in getting Jerrick shot, he might have wanted to wait until I was here to do it. That way he stays nice and safe and snuggly."

"Then what'd you ask what I thought for?"

Recker shrugged again. "Figured I'd be nice and give you a say. You do live here."

"And what if I said to leave them alone?"

"I just would've done what I wanted, anyway."

Tyrell rolled his eyes and sighed. "You're impossible sometimes, you know that?"

"If only I had a dollar for every time I'd heard that."

"Yeah, you'd have more money than Bill Gates by now, wouldn't ya?"

Recker smiled. "Probably."

"How long you gonna wait?"

"No time like the present. Chris, you ready to do this thing?"

"Ready when you are. How you wanna play it?"

"Well I can't just walk over to one of them. They'll get antsy as soon as I get near them. Gonna have to make it look like I left and then sneak back up on them."

"We can try to time it."

"They're not looking for you so you can probably stay in your car. Give me a few minutes. I'll let you know when I'm ready."

"Roger that."

"Well, I'm getting inside before all the shooting starts," Tyrell said.

"Probably a good idea."

"Call me if you need me. But not tonight."

Recker went back to his car and got inside, quickly driving off. He really wasn't sure if the men in the cars were going to follow him, though. If they did, he'd have to come up with a new plan. They didn't though. They stayed in their spots without moving an inch. After Recker turned off the street, he found another spot to park and quickly jumped out. He put his hand on his gun, though he didn't remove it yet. At that time of night, he didn't have to worry too much about onlookers, though there was always the possibility of a police cruiser coming by.

"Chris, starting my approach now."

"What if they recognize you walking?"

"I'm hoping they're not that observant as to what I was wearing."

Recker walked down the sidewalk toward the car, a dozen other cars lined up in back and in front of it. He wiped his hand on the side of his pants to get the sweat off of it before placing it back on his gun. When he was a couple of cars away, he let Haley know he was close.

"Chris, head up now."

"On the way."

Recker slowed down his pace a little until he saw the lights of Haley's car come zooming up the street. He then walked more swiftly to the car, putting his face down to make sure no one in the car could recognize him if they spotted him in the side mirror. Haley's car came to a sudden stop right next to the car that he had targeted. The occupants of the car immediately looked over at him and knew something was up. They scrambled for their weapons, but Haley immediately opened fire, shattering pieces of glass as the bullets ripped through the window until they found their final resting spots within the men's bodies.

As soon as the shots were heard, the other men closer to Recker, jumped out of their cars, ready to join the fight. Recker immediately raised his weapon and fired two shots at the passenger, drilling him in the back. The driver turned around, just barely long enough to see Recker's face before he too dropped to the ground. Recker didn't have to check on their status. He knew they were dead.

"Let's get out of here," Recker said.

Haley continued driving down the street, at first speeding off to make sure no one saw him, not that it would have really mattered if they copied his fake license plate, but once he was off the street, he drove at a normal pace once again. Recker ran back to his car as well, quickly jumping in and driving away.

"Looks like mission accomplished," Haley said.

"Yeah, for now."

"Wonder if that'll start something."

"Oh, it'll start something," Recker said. "It's just a question of what."

15

Recker was waiting for his guest to arrive, passing the time by walking along the Delaware River. It was a cool day, and slightly windy, but this was where Vincent wanted to meet. It was Recker who requested the meeting, but he had a feeling Vincent wanted to get a few things off his chest as well. He waited about twenty minutes before Vincent finally showed up. The crime boss came walking down the path, Malloy closely following behind him. There were quite a few more men that set up a distance away from each other, almost like it was a presidential guard, making sure no one interrupted.

"My apologies for being late," Vincent said. "Things are always coming up."

"Thanks for making the time."

"Always for you. What's this about?"

"I don't want to be lied to or misled," Recker

answered. "I think we're past that now, don't you?"

"Of course."

"Did you know this Jerrick was in town?"

Vincent sighed and took a few seconds to respond. "So you know who it is now?"

"Question is, how long have you known?"

"Not as long as you're assuming."

"But you did know?"

"Let me set the stage for you. About five or six months ago, I started getting word about there being a new player in town. Now, that in itself isn't exactly big news. In a city this big, in which I'm in control of most of it, there's always someone new popping in and trying to get a piece of the pie. It's a regular occurrence."

"You didn't know who it was at first?"

"No. Not for quite a while, actually. It was a big mystery, really hush-hush. Just a lot of talk about this new mystery player who was recruiting hard."

"When did you know?"

"It really wasn't until Jimmy told me about Tyrell being taken until I put it all together."

"But you knew the name?"

"Yes. I heard the name Jerrick. Didn't really mean much to me at the time I heard it. This wasn't until a few weeks ago, until I even got that piece of information. It's been very secretive up to now."

"Why didn't you tell me then?"

"I didn't think it pertained to you at that time. All I

heard for months was that there was a new guy in town, that he was assembling an organization, that everyone thought he was gunning for me. I didn't have a name, didn't have any ideas on what his plans were, nothing. Then when Sadko quit, that's when it really hit me that I had to be concerned."

"He knew everything about your schedule. Everything inside."

"He knows the way we operate, the places we go, the people we see, everything. I mean, he wasn't high on the totem pole or anything, but still, he knows things most people don't. So then, I really started turning the heat up, trying to find out who this guy was. I knew it wasn't as simple as Justin starting his own group. He wouldn't have the wherewithal to pull something like this off. He's got the brawn, but not the brains."

"So what'd you do?"

"As soon as Sadko left, I immediately changed everything. Stopped going to familiar places, changed up meeting places and times, did business completely differently. If there's a new guy in town who's now got one of my guys, he could surprise me very easily at a hundred different places and take me out. This is why I've been meeting in unorthodox places for me lately. Have to change habits."

Recker nodded. "I've been wondering why Jerrick hasn't taken his shot at you before now. He missed his best chance at it when he recruited Sadko."

"I agree. And I knew that. And it made me very uncomfortable. That's why I changed routines immediately. I knew his best chance to hurt me was to get me when I was vulnerable, which was in the days and weeks after Sadko left. Before then, he was still gathering men, beginning his plans, but once he got Justin, that was his opportunity to strike. And he would have if I hadn't changed course."

"Makes sense."

"Then a week, two weeks, three weeks ago, whatever it was, I finally got word about this Jerrick figure. Still not much about him, just a name, that maybe he was behind everything."

"What'd you do?"

"I did what I would do with anyone. We started investigating, seeing what we could find out on this Jerrick, figuring out if he had ties to anyone."

"Did you know he had ties to Jeremiah?"

"Not at first. It was actually Jimmy who remembered there was a Jerrick that was in Jeremiah's gang. As you know, we had checks on all of his men when Jeremiah was operating, knew who all his men were."

"You didn't put the name together at first?"

"Not at first, no. When Jeremiah was eliminated, I thought all his men had died with him. I didn't get word that any of his men had left town before that."

"Neither did I," Recker said.

"Then we did some digging and found out this Jerrick was the same guy on Jeremiah's crew."

"What do you know about him?"

"Not much. Jeremiah was high on him apparently, thought he could eventually take over the business in ten years or whenever Jeremiah was ready to step aside. But when he was here, Jerrick was no more than a mid-level guy. He wasn't high up in the organization."

"Jerrick told me that Jeremiah sent him away to start his own gang and learn the ropes, that way when he came back he'd move in without missing a beat."

"Quite possible."

"You didn't put the connections together when I told you someone was after me?"

"No. At that time, I had no reason to believe it was the same person. We hadn't gotten any information that Jerrick was also after you. As far as we believed, his only interest was moving in on me. When you said someone had taken a shot at you, and went to your apartment, and even with Mia, for that matter, I had just assumed that it was a different person. There was no evidence that it was all Jerrick behind everything."

"Maybe that's why he started on me," Recker said. "He wasn't getting what he wanted when he brought Sadko on board. Maybe his initial intention was to get Sadko, then ambush you, then he'd take over. With you changing everything, that inside information was not as helpful as he wanted, so he had to change course."

Vincent nodded, agreeing with the assessment. "So he remembers from the last time he was here that Mia worked at the hospital and that she was involved with you. He picks up from where Jeremiah left off in trying to use her to get to you. He knows you have a relationship with me, and eventually, he'll get to me through you. But at the same time, he still wants to take you out for what happened before. So now, he gets to you, brings me out of the light, and he gets to start trying to pick us apart."

"So initially, he follows her, finding out where we live. Sees us go downtown, tries to take the shot at me. Then when he misses, he goes to our apartment to try and find out if I've got any addresses or phone numbers written down of you, or Jones, or anything they can find. If he can, that's where he takes his next shot."

"But he can't find anything, so then he resorts to his next option. It's back to the hospital to try and take your girl. I believe his plan wasn't to kill her. At least not at first. I think he was going to take her to try and lure you out."

"Probably."

"But then that failed as well, so then he had to go and take Tyrell. He knew Ty had an arrangement with both of us, and that was his way back in. So when Jimmy told me that Tyrell had been kidnapped, and they wanted to use that as a way to meet with you... I knew it was Jerrick. I knew it was him behind everything. That's when all the little missing pieces all started fitting together. That's when I knew." Recker nodded, believing him. "Believe me, if I knew about this months ago, and knew that you were a target, and that Mia was a target, I wouldn't have kept it from you."

Recker looked at him and nodded again. "I believe it."

Vincent then patted Recker on the shoulder. "Now, there may have been a few people I know that I wouldn't have given the same courtesy to, but they're little weasels, hardly warranting the gesture. But not you. You deserve that respect."

"Well, the question now is where does Jerrick go from here? Where do we go from here? When I took Tyrell home last night, I saw a couple of Jerrick's men outside watching his place."

"Are they still there?"

"No. We took care of them."

"The best way we can probably deal with Jerrick now is to bring him out into the light. Find a way to make him show himself and stop operating in the shadows."

"That's gonna be difficult. He's a Jeremiah disciple, but he doesn't operate the same way. Jeremiah operated by brute force and dared you to stop him. He didn't care if you knew where he was or if he was coming. Jerrick doesn't seem to operate like that. At least not so far. He's been relying on finesse, out thinking you, catching you off-guard. He'll know we're trying to lure him out. He won't take the bait so easily."

"I agree. But until we have something else to hang our hats on, it's going to be our best bet."

"It won't happen quickly."

Vincent sighed, not liking the possibility of a long struggle, but agreeing it was the most realistic outcome. "No. I think we'll be in this for the long haul."

"Looks like we'll both have to be on guard at all times for the next little while. We'll have to be at the top of our game."

Vincent nodded. "Every thing we do, every operation we have, every person we talk to, they all could be a Jerrick plant. Everything we do could be being manipulated by him to catch us in a compromising situation. And that's when he'll take his next shot."

"Can you still lend a few men at the hospital in case he tries there again?"

"Absolutely. Consider it done. They're there for as long as you need them. But do you really think he'll try there again?"

Recker looked out at the river, watching the water get moved around by the wind gusts. He tried to put himself in Jerrick's shoes. "Not at first. I think he'll try some alternative measures first. But I don't think he would wait too long to try it again. Not if he feels he doesn't have many other options. And now that he's made himself visible, now that he knows we're both on to him, I don't think he's going to wait that long to strike. He'll want to get in the first blow. And he'll want to do it soon."

As Recker and Vincent walked along the banks of the river, Malloy answered a phone call. He stopped walking as he concentrated on what he was being told. He stood still for a minute, making sure he understood completely what was going on. After the call was over, he jogged forward to catch up with the others, eventually catching them and whispering in Vincent's ear. The look of concern on Vincent's face was unmistakable as he glared at his trusty lieutenant. Vincent thought for a few seconds about how to proceed.

"Bring the car around."

Malloy instantly turned and motioned to one of the other men, giving him hand signals to bring the cars up near where they were.

"Everything all right?" Recker asked.

"It appears Jerrick's plans are happening even sooner than we anticipated."

"What's going on?"

"Four of my men were ambushed twenty minutes ago outside of one of our businesses."

"They make it?"

"They're dead. I have to go and figure out what happened."

"I understand."

Before he left, Vincent left him with one last piece of advice. "From here on out, if either one of us get anything, no matter how small or insignificant, we'll share it with the other. Agreed?"

Recker nodded and shook his hand. "Agreed."

"Together, we'll find this son of a bitch and bury him."

16

Recker had just reached the office. Haley was at a computer. Jones was swiveling around from station to station. Something was going on.

"Should I ask?" Recker said.

"Don't get too comfortable," Jones replied.

"Why?"

"We may have a job coming up."

"I take it that means soon."

"Most likely. Where have you been?"

"Meeting with Vincent," Recker answered. "Told you I was meeting him this morning."

"I didn't realize it would take so long."

"Had to set up a different spot. Four of his men got ambushed while we were talking." Jones and Haley stopped what they were doing and turned to face him. "Not right where we were. While we were talking, he got word his men got ambushed somewhere else."

"Oh. Serious?"

"Dead."

"I'm guessing I should take it that our new friend Jerrick is somehow involved."

"I think that would be a good assumption. What do we have going on here?"

"Robbery attempt."

"How bad?"

"Aren't they all equal levels of bad?"

"Well..." Recker sighed. "With everything else we got going on..."

"The world doesn't stop just because we're having a rough time of it."

"I'm aware of that."

"Nobody is going to feel sorry for us."

"Didn't say they would."

"We still have to fight crime on multiple levels."

"I know."

"I just thought I'd mention it."

"Thanks. Appreciate the pep talk, Dad."

After a few more minutes of scrambling between computer screens, Jones finally got the last piece of information that he needed.

"There it is," Jones said, writing down the time. "Thirty minutes." He ripped the paper off the legal pad and handed it to Recker.

"What is it?"

"Jewelry store robbery. The store's located in a strip center. It's on the end of eight buildings."

Recker sighed. "Of course it is." Recker continued reading the paper. Seeing the address, he knew they could make it there in fifteen minutes. There was time to digest what he was reading first. "Four guys." He lowered the paper to his waist. "Any chances of surprises this time?"

"Not that I'm aware of. I'm fairly confident it's only four."

"Fairly confident, huh? Just fairly?"

Jones threw his hands up. "What do you want from me? I only work here."

Recker snickered. "All look like they've done some time."

"But none so much that they look like they should give you problems."

"We'll see about that."

Recker sighed again and put the paper in his pocket. He looked at Haley. "You ready to roll?"

Haley was already getting guns out of the cabinet, including the ones that he knew Recker liked to use. He closed the doors. "Let's do it."

Recker and Haley hurried out of the office and jumped into Recker's car. They didn't feel the need to go separately in this instance. Everything seemed like it was happening at the same place. As they drove to the jewelry store, they began formulating their plan.

"What are you thinking?" Haley asked.

"Uh, I'm thinking we could both be inside, posing

as customers when they come in. Then as soon as they flash their guns, we take them out."

"What if they keep someone outside? Either on the door or in a car?"

"We either let them skate or one of us stays outside and keeps watch."

"I'm thinking we do one in, one out. That way we cover all our bases."

"And if they all go in?"

"Whoever's watching the outside goes in after them."

"Could get caught in the crossfire."

"Could happen anyway."

"True," Recker said. "All right, you wanna do it that way?"

"I think that's the best move."

Recker nodded. "Which spot you want?"

"Don't matter."

"I'll take inside and you take outside?"

"Works for me."

They arrived at the jewelry store roughly ten minutes before the incident was about to go down. They stayed in their car for a minute and just looked around, making sure the crew wasn't there already, waiting for their cue to go in. They didn't see anyone waiting in a car that was nearby, though.

"Where you gonna set up?" Recker asked.

Haley quickly looked around. He had a straight

view to the store from where they were sitting. "I dunno. Looks like right here's pretty good."

"What if they drive up in a van or something and it blocks your view?"

Haley shrugged. "Then I'll move."

Recker shrugged as well. He was good with it. If he was on an assignment with someone else, a rookie, or just someone he didn't know or trust as well as Haley, he might have wanted some more assurances than that. After all, it was Recker's life on the line if he was in the store with men firing guns at him. But Haley was a pro's pro, and Recker didn't have to worry about him ever not being where he was supposed to be.

"Keep com's on?" Recker asked.

Haley nodded as he grabbed his weapon and touched his ear. "On."

Recker swiveled his head around to scan the parking lot as he walked toward the jewelry store, just in case the crew came in hot and heavy. Once he made it to the doors, he opened them, and found the store was pretty light on customers. There was a man behind the counter dealing with an elderly couple, and another woman, younger, mid-thirties, on the opposite side of the store, helping out another woman near the same age.

"Be right with you, sir," the male worker said, looking at the door as the bell rang when Recker stepped inside. "As soon as I'm finished with these fine folks, I'll be right there."

"Take your time," Recker said.

As he waited for the action to come, Recker walked around the glass counters, looking inside them at the merchandise. After looking at a few pieces, he almost forgot why he was actually there. He looked back at the door, then at the time. It was right when the crew was supposed to get there.

"How we looking out there?"

"Quiet as can be for now," Haley answered. "Nothing moving. I take it nobody's in there already?"

"No, only three customers in here."

"Could one be an advance scout?"

Recker carefully looked at the three customers. "No, I don't think so. I don't get that vibe. They just seem like regular people."

Haley's eyes glanced at a white van pulling into the parking lot. It was unmarked. And it looked like it could use a wash, though it wasn't the dirtiest he'd ever seen.

"Wait, this might be it. White van."

Recker took his eyes off the people and tried to look through the windows, though it was a little tougher to see with the bars on them. A few seconds later, he saw the van pulling up in front of the store and stopping.

"I see it," Recker said.

The doors opened up, with three men jumping out of the back. They put black ski masks on just before they entered the store. Recker turned his body slightly to ready himself and get into a position to fire. He removed his gun and held it by his leg, his body shielding it from the view of anyone who walked through that door.

"Looks like one's staying in the van," Haley said.

Haley got out of the car and started moving around a few other cars, trying to come up on the van through a blind spot near the corner of the bumper of it. The door to the store finally opened, the little bell ringing to signify a new customer. When everyone looked over, they were horrified to see three men with guns and masks on. Everyone immediately started to panic and put their hands up.

"All right, this is a robbery," the leader said. "Everyone calm down, do what you're told, and nobody gets hurt." The other two walked in, pointing their guns at people. The leader of the group pointed his gun at the male clerk. "You, start putting money and jewelry into these bags." He had several duffel bags strapped around his shoulder. He put them on the counter.

As the clerk started to comply with the robber's wishes, the leader of the group looked over at Recker. He had a bad feeling about him. He didn't look as worried as the others. Recker had a calm look on his face. It wasn't natural for someone to be in this type of situation and not be worried.

"You, get on the floor," the leader said.

Recker shook his head. "No, don't think I will."

"I said get on the floor!"

The man started to turn his gun in Recker's direction, but Recker just swung his gun around and started blasting away without further provocation. The leader of the group got two bullets in his chest for starters, knocking him onto the ground. A couple of screams were heard from the customers, and the workers, who all quickly dropped to the floor to try and get out of the way of any flying projectiles. Recker quickly got off a few shots at the leader's buddies, each of whom also received a bullet for their troubles. The shots were heard outside the store, and the driver of the van jumped out of the car to see what was going on. As soon as he did, he saw Haley coming up from behind. The driver reached for his weapon, which was tucked away inside the belt of his pants, but Haley beat him to the punch and quickly dispersed of him.

Inside the store, one of the men had survived the initial bullet, and tried to stand back up. He grabbed his weapon and got to one knee, but it was short-lived, and Recker finished the man off by putting another bullet in his chest. There were still a few screams that could be heard by Haley outside the store. With his man out of the way, Haley went inside, peeking his head in to make sure it didn't get blasted off his shoulders first. Seeing Recker standing there without a worried look on his face, he knew it was safe to go in. Haley stepped over one of the bodies and looked at the damage. He was surprised that none of the cases had been shot up or broken.

"Looks clean."

Recker shrugged. "Good aim."

"I meant by them."

"Oh. Never got a shot off."

Haley nodded, impressed. "Guy outside too."

Recker looked around at the other people in the store. "Everybody good?"

Everyone began standing back up again, checking themselves to make sure they weren't hurt, injured, or cut by something. The male clerk looked at everyone else and then spoke up.

"I think we're all good. Thank you."

Recker nodded at him. "Glad to help."

"Are you with the police?"

"Uh... different agency. Basically on the same team though."

The clerk took a deep breath. "I can't believe they were going to try and rob us."

"Happens quite a bit."

"I just... can't believe it. I've never been through something like this before."

"Well, hope you never have to go through it again."

"Ready?" Haley asked.

Recker took a few steps towards the door, then looked back at one of the glass cases. He walked back over to it. He looked at something that caught his eye.

He saw a necklace that interested him, then pointed to it.

"Could I see that?"

The clerk walked over to the case and unlocked it. "See something you like?"

"Maybe."

As it looked like they were carrying on with their day like nothing ever happened, Haley looked down at the dead bodies on the floor. He shrugged. "Usual day at the office, I guess."

The clerk took out the necklace and handed it to Recker for him to inspect it. "It really is a lovely piece. Do you have someone you think would like it?"

"Uh, yeah," Recker answered. "I think she would. How much is it?"

"It is only nine hundred dollars."

"Nine hundred, huh?"

"Yes, it's actually quite a bargain. It's on sale at the moment. It regularly retails for over fifteen hundred."

Haley was starting to squirm a little. He kept looking out the window, waiting for the police to arrive. "Hey, uh, you think we should get moving here? I mean, there are these guys on the floor and all."

Recker didn't bother to look at him, instead, keeping his focus on the necklace. "We still got time. We got a few minutes."

Though Haley wasn't of the jumpy sort by nature, he knew when the clock was ticking. And it was getting near the alarm right now. He cleared his throat and looked out the window again. It wasn't often that Recker bought something like this for Mia, but she deserved it. She deserved more than he gave her. But he knew she would like this.

"Yeah. Yeah, I'll take it."

"Excellent choice, sir," the clerk said. "Let me just put it in the box for you."

The two went over to the register, where Recker paid by credit card. Haley started tapping his foot on the floor, hoping they would hurry it up. He put his hand on his face, feeling like trouble was coming any second. Once the necklace was paid for, Recker put the small box in his pocket and walked over to his partner.

"Uh, excuse me, sir," the clerk said, putting his finger in the air. "But, uh, what are we going to do about... them?" He then pointed to the bodies on the floor.

Recker looked down at them. "Oh, them? Don't worry about it. The police will be here in a few minutes to mop things up. Thanks." Recker gave them a salute as he and Haley walked out of the store.

The clerk's mouth fell open, unsure of everything that just happened. "Uh... thank you... I guess."

As Recker and Haley got near the car, Recker tossed his partner his keys and jumped in the passenger seat. As they pulled out of the parking lot, several police cruisers pulled in.

Haley loudly sighed and shook his head. "That was close. Too close. Did you have to go shopping now?"

"What?" Recker held the necklace up. "Mia will like this, don't you think?"

"She'll love it. Did you have to make it so close though?"

"What, told you we had time."

"Is there a specific reason you had to get that?"

"No. Nothing other than she's the best."

"Well I'll agree with you there."

They were about halfway back to the office when Recker's phone rang. He looked over at Haley.

"It's Malloy," Recker said. He then answered it. "How's it going?"

There was no immediate response, but judging by what Recker heard in the background, he could tell how it was going. He heard voices yelling and screaming, what sounded like guns being fired, and he even thought he detected an explosion, though he couldn't say for certain.

"Uh, is everything all right?" Recker asked.

There was a brief pause before Malloy's voice was finally heard. "No!"

Recker heard more gunfire. "What's happening?"

"We're pinned down. Need help. Can you get here?"

"Where you at?" As Malloy rattled off the address, Recker tapped his partner on the arm and motioned for him to turn the car around. They were headed in the wrong direction.

"What's going on?"

"Too much to talk. Just get here!"

"We're on the way. Give us twenty."

After Recker put his phone down, Haley wondered about what was happening. "Where we going?"

"Looks like one of Vincent's warehouses."

"What for?"

Recker shrugged. "Didn't say. Some kind of trouble. Sounded urgent. Said they were pinned down."

"Who? Just him?"

"Didn't say. Judging by what was happening in the background, didn't sound like it. Sounded like the whole platoon was there."

"Who they up against?"

"Don't know. Maybe it's Jeremiah's men."

"You mean Jerrick."

"Oh, yeah," Recker said. "One and the same seems like."

"So what are we, the reinforcements?"

"Seems like. When I left that meeting with Vincent, they said his men had been ambushed. They went off to check it out. I'm guessing this is the result of that."

"Looks like it was a bigger ambush than they thought."

"Looks like."

"Guess we're the cavalry."

Recker nodded. "Off to save the day again."

17

Vincent and Malloy were taking cover behind their car, keeping their heads down as much as possible to avoid them getting shot off. They periodically rose up over it to get off a few shots of their own.

"I'm not sure we can hold them off until Recker gets here," Malloy said.

"We just need to keep them at bay for now," Vincent replied. "We don't need to take wild shots and try to take them all out now. We just need to keep them busy."

Malloy looked past his boss at one of the other cars, which also had two of their men behind it, in the same situation that they were in. "I'd say it's more of them keeping us busy."

He then looked back to his left, where there was another car with two men behind it. That was all they had left. The six of them. When they first arrived at the warehouse, upon hearing that four of their men had been ambushed there, there were twelve of them. Four of them went down on the second ambush. The other two were lost during the subsequent fight, which was still going. They never had a chance. As soon as they rolled up on the scene and started looking at their fallen comrades, the second round of fighting started, picking off some of them immediately. Only a minute or two later, another one of them went down. The bullet appeared to come from the side this time.

"They're starting to flank us!" Malloy yelled.

"We're gonna have to get inside," Vincent said.

Malloy turned his head to see how far it was to the warehouse. It was a good thirty yards or so to the door. And it was a wide open space between that and the cars.

"I don't think we're all gonna be able to make it. They'll pick a few of us off."

"It's better than them picking all of us off here," Vincent replied.

Malloy looked to the car to their right, which now only had one man behind it. "Hey, John! We're gonna make a run for the warehouse! Move to our car first and I'll try and cover you!"

The man instantly made a dash for the car Vincent and Malloy were behind. As soon as he started running, Malloy rose up and started firing where he thought their attackers were, even though he couldn't see any of them. All he was trying to do was make them duck their heads while the bullets were flying to give their man a chance. Once their man made it safely to the car, Malloy looked to the other car.

"Guys!" Malloy pointed to the warehouse. "Start making your way there! We'll try and cover you from there! Then when you get there, you cover us!"

The men nodded, understanding the plan. They immediately ran toward the warehouse, with Vincent, Malloy, and the other man all firing to try and cover them. After a few seconds, Malloy looked back to see if their men had made it. One of them had. The other was lying face down, motionless.

Malloy sighed. "Lost another one."

"We can't worry about that now," Vincent said. "It's our turn to move."

Malloy tapped the other man on the shoulder to give him the plan. "We let Vincent get ahead of us. We'll stick right behind him and try to cover him as much as possible. I don't want them to get an easy shot at him." The man nodded. "We'll turn around once or twice to give him more time to get there." The man nodded again, good with the plan. "You ready, boss?"

"Let's go," Vincent replied.

Vincent rose to his feet and took off toward the warehouse. Malloy and the other man stood up and started firing wildly. The man already at the warehouse did the same. After a couple of seconds, Malloy and the other man ran towards Vincent. Once they caught up to him, they both turned around and started firing again. Just as they were about to turn back and start running again, Malloy's partner bent over and clutched his stomach. Malloy saw him hunch over and went over to him to help him, but just as he got there, another bullet penetrated the man's torso, sending him to the ground. Malloy knew he was gone. All he could do now was help himself. He dropped to a knee and continued firing blindly. He turned his head around to look at the warehouse and saw that Vincent had made it safely.

"Jimmy!" Vincent yelled. "C'mon! We'll cover you!"

Malloy quickly got back to his feet and sprinted toward the warehouse. As he did, Vincent and the last remaining man fired furiously, hoping that one of their badly aimed bullets would be lucky enough to hit something. They didn't, but it did happen to be enough to get Malloy to the warehouse unscathed. Just as he reached it, the other man burst through the front door to open it, Vincent and Malloy following him inside. Once in there, they immediately took up spots by windows.

Malloy was still breathing heavily. "That should at least buy us a few minutes."

Vincent looked at the time. He was concerned, but not yet worried. He knew Recker and Haley should have been arriving any minute. If they weren't coming, he might have felt like the walls were closing in. But he wasn't at that point yet. Right before Malloy called Recker, he called more of Vincent's men, but they were farther away conducting other business, and while they were coming, they were likely at least five or ten minutes behind Recker.

"We just need to hold them off for a few more minutes," Vincent said.

"When's Recker getting here? Should be here by now."

"Patience, my friend. He'll be here. He may be already."

"How you figure?"

"If I know him, just because we can't see him, doesn't mean he can't see us. He may be out there stalking his prey."

"Man, I sure hope so," Malloy said. "Depending on how many people they got out there, if they start rushing us, I'm not sure how much longer we can hold out."

"Just have to give them a few more minutes."

Malloy checked his weapon and had a new concern. "I'm running out of ammo. Only have one mag left." He looked to the other man. "What about you? What do you have left?"

"I got two."

"Make every shot count. Can't spray and pray."

Recker and Haley had pulled up just in front of the gate that led to the warehouse. It was closed and locked, which made them get out and look for an alternate entry point. They grabbed a pair of bolt cutters and walked around to the side of the property, finding a piece of the tall chain-link fence that they could cut through to make their entrance. Once they crawled through, they immediately heard gunfire coming from their right. Recker motioned to Haley about splitting up, with Recker continuing to follow along the fence, while Haley would move around some shipping containers.

As Recker and Haley merged closer to their targets, the sound of guns firing grew a little bit louder. They were close. They just had to find the exact spots of the shooters. After a few more seconds, they found the first one. They were on opposite sides of one of the containers, and Recker looked up, identifying one of the men as being on top of it. He couldn't see them yet, but they were there. He looked at Haley, then pointed at himself, and made a motion with his fingers that he was going to go up on top of the container. Haley nodded, then started looking around to give his partner protection in case someone else came along, so Recker didn't have to worry about anyone other than the man on top.

Recker slowly climbed the ladder on the side of the container, making sure he didn't make any noises that would give away his presence. Surprise would be his ally here. As he reached the top of the ladder, Recker peeked his head over the side of the container, seeing a man lying flat on his stomach with an automatic rifle. He was positioned away from Recker, so he didn't see him coming. Recker pushed himself up on top of the container, making the slightest of noises as his handle of his gun brushed up against the metal container. It made the shooter flinch and look back. Upon seeing the strange man standing there, he rolled over and tried to get a shot off, though Recker fired three rounds that all landed before the man could do the same to him. That shooter was gone, but Recker looked over at the other dozen containers that were lined up to the right of the one he was standing on, and saw four more shooters spaced out.

"Oh, crap," Recker said, observing the four men all turn to look at him.

The bullets came only a few seconds later. Recker immediately dropped to his stomach and quickly slithered his way back down the ladder, giving the shooters as small a target to shoot at as possible. Once back on the ground, he and Haley came up with a new plan.

"There's four guys up there," Recker said. "Spaced out."

"Well they got nowhere to go. No need to rush and do anything stupid."

Recker wiped his mouth with his forearm, trying to think of what to do. "True. But we also don't know if they're it or there's more roaming around here. This is a big place. I wouldn't be surprised if there's more somewhere else. I just don't want us to get trapped by someone coming up from behind us while they're shooting at us from above."

"I kind of doubt Vincent and Malloy got pinned

down with just five shooters. Especially all at one angle. I'd assume they were shooting from different positions."

Recker nodded. "Yeah, I'd agree. Question is, where are the rest?"

"Let's just knock out these guys first. Take it one at a time."

"Well, we got them at a disadvantage. In order to fire at us, they gotta reveal themselves. They can't just lay there. They gotta get up, and when they do, they'll give us a target."

They sprinted over to the next container. Recker stopped short of it, standing at the previous container to give himself a good line of fire. Haley kept going until he got to the one the next shooter was on. He made sure he banged against the container to make sure the shooter knew someone was there. It worked. The man on top looked down to see who was there, giving Recker just enough of a target to fire. Upon the bullet entering the man's body, he fell limp and fell forward off the container, hitting the ground with a thump.

The plan worked well, so they decided to try it again with the next one. They did the same exact thing. And just like the last one, the plan worked to perfection. With two more shooters to go, though, they weren't about to fall prey to the same trick. After seeing the first three guys go down, the last two weren't waiting for the same fate. They immediately started climbing down off their respective containers. Recker and Haley were waiting for the first man as his feet touched the ground, both of them hitting the unsuspecting man at the same time.

Several bullets ricocheted off the containers behind them as the final man reached the ground and spotted them and began firing. Haley dropped to the ground on his stomach as he returned fire, while Recker took cover behind the next container. There was a brief back-and-forth exchange which only lasted about thirty seconds before the last man was also terminated.

Recker and Haley met up again by the edge of the container and started looking around to figure out their next move. It was quickly determined for them, though. Several more shots rang out, though they were farther away.

"Sounds like maybe it's coming from the other side," Haley said.

Recker agreed. "Probably holed up in the warehouse."

Recker and Haley started running for the warehouse, weaving between a couple of containers on the way there. They wanted to get there quickly, but at the same time, not make any sloppy mistakes on the way there like making themselves a highly visible target. It was only a couple of minutes before the warehouse was in sight. Once they ran past the containers, it wasn't just a straight path to the warehouse, though.

There were plenty of other storage boxes, crates, and equipment along the way. It almost felt like it was staged the way it was set up. It wasn't an abandoned facility, though. There was actually work done there from time to time. Vincent did make sure there were plenty of obstacles around, as he usually did in the places that he owned, so that it did afford him some protection in the event something like this ever happened. He never wanted to be caught out in the open with nowhere to go.

Once the warehouse was in their sights, Recker and Haley immediately saw where the commotion was coming from. There were four men just on the outside of the warehouse shooting at targets inside, which they figured was where Vincent and his team had retreated to. Then one of the men broke off from the main group and started moving to the side.

Haley tapped Recker on the arm. "Hey, one guy's trying to move around!"

"He's yours, take him."

As Haley moved on from his position, Recker tried to move too, to get a little better line of sight on the remaining three guys. He didn't want to alert them of his presence yet, hoping he could take them by surprise and pick one or two of them off before they knew he was there. As he took up a new position, Haley quickly ran for the back, getting there just in time as the other man was trying to open the back door. The man saw Haley coming out of the corner of his eye and stopped what he was doing to face him. He jumped and turned to the side, pointing his gun, though he didn't get a chance to fire it before Haley took him out.

"Man down," Haley said.

"Good," Recker replied. "Just stay back there and cover that door in case there's more."

"Will do."

Haley retreated back to another spot on the perimeter so he could still keep an eye on the door if anyone else tried the same idea. Recker had now moved to a more advantageous position, getting a clear view of the sides of a couple of the men. As soon as he had a shot, he took it. The man closest to him immediately went down. Upon seeing their partner drop, the man in the middle instantly turned, a look of bewilderment on his face as he tried to understand what was happening. The look was quickly erased by one of pain as a slug from Recker's gun penetrated his torso. Once he dropped, the third remaining man of the group raised his body and started shooting at Recker's position, causing Recker to take cover behind a large crate. But in the process of firing, the man exposed himself to the warehouse, with all three men inside finding their mark at the same time.

There was an eerie silence that filled the air, as no one was quite sure that the battle was actually over, even though there were no more guns firing. Everyone just waited in their respective spots for the next few minutes, waiting for someone to move, someone to fire, a noise to be heard, something that would indicate there were more of them out there. But there wasn't. It was a noise that wouldn't come. After five more minutes, all the respective combatants started to leave their positions. Recker moved into the open in front of the warehouse, Vincent, Malloy, and their other man came out of the warehouse, and Haley emerged from the back of it. They all convened in a circle a few yards in front of the warehouse building. Vincent motioned to his man to check on all the bodies, both theirs, and their attackers, to see if anyone was still alive.

"I thank you for the assist," Vincent said.

Recker nodded. "Glad we were able to get here in time."

Malloy grinned. "Though you did cut it close."

"Better late than not at all."

"I won't argue with that."

"What exactly happened?"

Vincent took a deep breath before he answered. "Well, as you know from our meeting this morning when I told you our men had been ambushed, this was where it happened. We came up on the scene, started checking my guys, then more bullets ripped through the sky. And more of my men went down." Vincent's eyes naturally looked to the ground, where he saw a few of his men laying. There was an obvious sadness to his face.

"How'd they know about this place?"

"Sadko," Malloy answered. "Had to be."

Vincent nodded. "Yes. I would agree. He's been here. He knew of it."

"How would he know your guys would be here though?" Recker asked.

"Even if we're not conducting business somewhere, we still maintain checks on all of our properties regularly. I send out teams to check places, make sure there are no vagrants, nobody's broken in, things like that. Since this is a facility we're still using on a fairly regular basis, it gets checked every week."

"Every Wednesday it's been," Malloy said.

Vincent sighed. "Yeah. Every Wednesday. We've moved a lot of our deals around to be more unpredictable, show up at different places and different times, but this... with this we got sloppy."

"It's my fault. I should've changed the schedule."

"No, Jimmy, I allowed it to go. I figured they would be more preoccupied with cutting in on some of our deals that I didn't think they would worry about building checks. Such a mundane task. Show up to a place, check it out, leave five or ten minutes later."

"Five minutes is all it takes," Recker said. "You don't think this could be someone else, other than Sadko?"

"No."

"It's definitely him," Malloy said.

"The real question is whether he's doing it on his own or under Jerrick's orders."

"I would think it's with Jerrick's blessing. From my

brief conversation with him, I got the impression he runs a tight ship. I don't think he gives his guys free-lancing capabilities. He does what he wants, when he wants. And there's no deviations."

A minute later, the rest of Vincent's men arrived through the gate, finding the group in front of the warehouse. Vincent instructed them to search the rest of the grounds to make sure there was no one else still there lying in the weeds. Then Vincent's other man came over to him.

"Everyone's dead, sir."

"Even our guys?" Malloy asked. "None are still breathing."

"Everyone's dead. Everyone."

Vincent looked at his top lieutenant with a worried look on his face. "It appears a formidable foe has grown within our mists. And a deadly one."

18

Recker and Haley were getting ready to leave the apartment when Recker suddenly remembered he had forgotten something. They arrived late the night before and Mia had fallen asleep on the couch waiting for them, so Recker didn't have the opportunity to give her the present yet. They had already said their goodbyes to Mia and had opened the door to leave when Recker tapped his friend on the arm.

"Wait a minute," Recker said. "I didn't give that necklace to Mia yet."

"Oh. You wanna do it now?"

"If you don't mind waiting."

Haley shrugged. "Don't matter to me. David said nothing's going on right now, so we got time."

As they walked back through the living room, Mia emerged from the kitchen. "What are you guys doing? Thought you were leaving?"

Recker put his finger in the air and disappeared into the hallway as he went into their bedroom.

"What's going on?" Mia asked. Haley shrugged again. "You know what this is about, don't you?"

"My lips are sealed."

Recker came back out a minute later, his arm tucked behind his back. He had a smile on his face. It actually made Mia a little suspicious and uncomfortable to see him act like that. It was unusual for him.

"What are you doing?" Mia asked.

She briefly looked at Haley before her eyes went back to her boyfriend. He was acting so strangely she had fleeting thoughts that, with one hand behind his back, he was about to get on one knee and ask her the question. She was starting to get nervous. Her thoughts were quickly put to rest when Recker suddenly brought his hand around, showing her a small box.

"Here," Recker said with a happy grin. "I got you something."

"You got me something? Why?"

Recker shrugged. "Just to let you know I love you and I appreciate you... just being you."

"Awe, that's so sweet." Mia then took the box from his hands and slowly opened it. She took out the necklace and held it up high, admiring it. "Wow, that is so pretty."

"You like it?"

"I love it." She then reached over and gave him a kiss and a hug. "It looks expensive."

"You're worth it."

Mia couldn't hide the smile from her face as she went over to a mirror and put it on. "I love it."

"You're not just saying that?"

Mia went back over to her boyfriend and jumped into his arms as she put her lips onto his. "I love it. And I love you thinking of me for no reason. When did you get this?"

"Just picked it up yesterday."

She put her hands on the side of his face and gave him another passionate kiss. "I love you."

"Love you too."

"Should I leave the room?" Haley asked, somewhat sarcastically.

Recker and Mia both looked over at him and smiled. The text ringer on Mia's phone then went off. She went over to it and made a small huffing sound.

"What is it?" Recker asked.

"Oh, just work. They wanted to know if I could come in today and cover a shift."

"But you're off today."

"Well, I'm not really doing anything, so I guess I can go in."

Recker shot Haley a look. "But we don't have coverage for you right now. Vincent's men aren't there."

"I'm sure I'll be fine."

"Mia..."

"Don't Mia me. I'm not gonna hide in a corner

somewhere. I'm sure they're not going to try the same thing again. You just go ahead and I'll be fine."

Recker shook his head. He wasn't having that. "No. Chris, why don't you head to the office? Tell David what's going on and I'll be in soon. If you need me for anything, call me."

"We got you covered," Haley said, leaving the apartment.

As Haley closed the door behind him, Recker gave Mia a face. She knew exactly what it meant.

"I can't just do nothing."

"I'm not saying to do nothing," Recker said. "I just want to make sure you're adequately protected."

"I'm fine. Nobody can get into that wing without proper credentials, anyway."

"We're not dealing with idiots here."

"They wouldn't try something there."

"Maybe. But last time they waited until you left."

"So I'll eat in the nurses' room."

Recker sighed, knowing he was going to lose the conversation. "Fine. But I'm driving you. And I'll pick you up."

"OK."

As Mia went into the bedroom to change and get ready, Recker made a phone call. Malloy immediately picked up.

"Hey, hate to bother you so soon after yesterday, but I got a question."

"Shoot," Malloy replied.

"Mia just got called into work. I know this wasn't on the schedule, and I know you guys are reeling a bit after losing some guys yesterday, but is there anyway you can still provide some coverage at the hospital today?"

Malloy thought for a few moments. "Uh, yeah, I think so. Might be a little bit of a scaled down crew though."

"Whatever you can give, I'd appreciate it."

"Might only be able to spare two or three guys today."

"Like I said, whatever you can give."

"Consider it done. When's she going in?"

"I'm driving her over in a few minutes."

"I can have them over there in about half an hour."

"Sounds good. I appreciate it."

"After what you did for us yesterday, it's the least we can do."

"How you guys making out?"

"We're dealing, you know? I mean, it's never easy burying guys you get close to, but I guess it's part of the deal, right?"

"It is."

"It's a small hit. A small setback. But we still got plenty of men. And we still got plenty of fight. We're going to bring it. And we're going to bring it soon."

"Hopefully this isn't something that drags out," Recker said. "I have a feeling that the longer this goes, the more powerful Jerrick's going to become. And it's going to get tougher to stop him."

"I agree. We'll get him."

Once Mia came back out, Recker quickly said goodbye and ended the conversation.

"Who was that?"

Recker shoved the phone into his pocket. "Uh, no one. Just... David."

"That was not David."

"How do you know?"

"Because I can always tell when you're talking to him."

"You can?"

"Yes."

"Well this time I was talking to him different."

"No you weren't. Don't lie to me."

Recker started to say something, but didn't want to keep lying, so he just threw his arms up.

"That was Vincent, wasn't it?"

"No."

"Malloy."

"Uh... maybe?"

"Mike, I'll be fine."

"I'm just making sure."

"You're having them send men there, aren't you?"

"Just a couple."

"Mike, you can't have people there twenty-four-seven."

"Who says?"

Mia rolled her eyes. "I know this is a fight I won't win, so I won't try anymore."

"Good. Because you weren't."

They left the apartment and drove down to the hospital. Mia was a bit surprised when he didn't pull up to the front to let her off. Recker parked in a spot.

"What are you doing?"

Recker turned the car off. "Walking you inside."

"I'm sure that's not necessary."

"Do I tell you how to take care of babies and new mothers in there?"

"No."

"Then don't tell me how to protect someone."

Mia rolled her eyes and sighed, but just accepted the answer and got out of the car. Recker walked her inside, keeping his head on a swivel as they walked in, ready and waiting for a surprise. Waiting for something to suddenly appear and jump out at them, probably holding a gun. Thankfully, nothing came. Once they got up to Mia's floor, they gave each other a hug and a kiss.

"I guess this is my stop," Mia said.

"Guess it is." They kissed again.

"I guess I'll let you know when I'm done."

Recker couldn't shake the feeling that something seemed off. He wasn't sure what it was. Nothing seemed out of the ordinary. The hospital seemed to be operating as it always did. But he still had that feeling that something was off.

"Would you stop worrying?" Mia said, knowing what the expression on his face meant.

"I'm just..."

"A worrywart. I'm fine. I'll be fine."

"I'm just... extra precautious. Especially when it comes to you."

"And I love you for it. But I'll be fine. Really. Now go do something. But try not to send anyone here when you do."

"Very funny."

"All right, I'm gonna go now."

"Wait." Recker took one last look around, still not shaking that feeling.

"What?"

"A code word."

"What?"

"A code word. Something you can give me to let me know if you get in trouble."

"Really, Mike?"

"I'm serious."

Mia leaned her head back. "Such as?"

"I don't know. If you get in trouble, just say something like, Dr. Recker is needed."

"Dr. Recker is needed? Seriously? Don't they already know your name?"

"Oh, yeah. Good point."

"Why don't I just mention the word Sunday?" Mia said it in a sarcastic tone, not believing she would ever have to use it.

"Sunday?"

"Yeah. If I say something with the word Sunday in it, it means I'm in trouble. OK?"

Recker sighed. "I guess that would work."

"Now I really should get in there. I'll call you when I'm done, OK?" Mia gave him a kiss.

As Recker went back down to the lobby, Mia clocked herself in and then went to the nurses' station. As she was sitting on the computer, checking the charts of a few patients that she was already familiar with, another nurse came over and sat down next to her.

"Hey, what are you doing here? Thought you were off today?"

Mia looked at her, dumbfounded, wondering why the other nurse was there. She was the nurse that Mia was supposed to be covering for.

"I was."

"They call you in?"

"Uh, yeah. Wait, they called me in for you."

"For me? I'm not going anywhere. I'm here. Why would they call you in for me?"

Mia scrunched her face together, not understanding what was going on. Mia pulled the phone out of her pocket and showed the nurse the message she got. "Look. Here. They said you weren't coming in."

"Hmm. That's weird. I never said I wasn't coming in."

Mia then walked around the floor until she found the nurse who was in charge of the scheduling.

"Hey, what are you doing here?" the nurse asked.

A red flag immediately shot up in Mia's head. She immediately pulled out her phone and showed her the message she got. "Didn't you send me this? It's your number."

The nurse didn't have any more of an idea as to what was happening than anyone else did. "That's weird. That's my number, but I didn't send you that." She then took out her own phone and looked at the text messages. She showed Mia. "Look. You're not there."

"Then why does it say from you? And who else would've sent it?"

The nurse shook her head, not having any answers. "I have no idea."

Panic started settling into Mia's head, thinking that she might have been tricked into coming there. She made a dash back to the nurses' station to grab her things, then quickly headed out the door, hoping she could catch Recker in time before he left. After she got off of the elevator on the first floor, she pulled out her phone as she raced down the hallway. A man opened a door and came out, bumping into Mia and sending her down to the ground, knocking the phone out of her hand.

"I'm terribly sorry," the man said.

"It's OK." Mia got back to her feet and looked around, searching for where her phone went.

The man put his hand on her arm. "Are you sure you're OK?"

"Uh, yeah, yeah, I'm fine." Mia barely even noticed him as she looked for her phone.

"Looking for this?" the man held up Mia's phone.

Mia stopped looking around and focused on the phone that was in the man's hand. It was hers. She barely even gave a glance to the man's face. "Thanks." She started to grab it, but the man pulled it away.

The man made a clicking noise with his mouth. "Not so fast. I think I'll just hold on to it for a bit."

"What? Give it to me."

Mia finally gave a good solid look to the man's face, recognizing who he was. It was Justin Sadko. She remembered seeing his picture the last time she was at the office when the gang was going over things. It was a face she wouldn't mistake.

Realizing she was in a lot of trouble, she took a step back and looked around. She looked like she was either about to run or scream. Either one was a problem for Sadko. He noticed her behavior and knew exactly what she was planning. He had to quickly put a stop to it.

"I wouldn't do that," Sadko said, putting his hand in the front pocket of his hoodie, intimating that he had a gun in there. "You scream, you run, and I'll just cut my losses right here and end you. There'll still be enough time for me to run out of here and get to my car before the police show up."

"Why? Why are you doing this? I don't even know you."

"Yeah, well, you have your boyfriend to thank for that."

"Why? What did he ever do to you? He barely even knows you."

"Hey, it's not personal. It's just business."

"What business is that?"

"With the type of men that are paying me, you don't ask questions. You just do the job."

"And that job is me?"

A half-smile came over Sadko's face. "Right now."

"I just... I don't understand."

"Luckily, you don't have to. But right now, you're coming with me."

"No."

"Listen, if I have to shoot you right here and now I will. I would rather not. But don't push me."

"If you're just going to take me somewhere else and kill me, I'm not going to make it easy for you."

"I'm not here to kill you. But I am here to take you with me. And you're coming."

"Why? Just so you can lure my boyfriend in so you can take him out too? I won't do it. I won't put him in jeopardy for me."

Sadko stepped in closer to her, their chests almost touching each other. He grew more agitated with each passing second they were there chatting. "You can and you will."

What seemed like a million thoughts ran through Mia's mind on how best to handle the situation. Her only thoughts at that moment were on how to help herself, while also protecting Recker from walking into an ambush in trying to save her. She wasn't sure she believed that Sadko would actually shoot her if she tried to run. But she didn't know the man well enough to know if he was bluffing either. Based on what she knew of him from Recker, it was possible he meant what he said. She didn't think she could take the chance. Even if she escaped, she wasn't sure if any stray bullets would hit anyone else roaming through the halls. She didn't want to put any innocent bystanders in peril either. Once she decided that going with Sadko was the best option, now her thoughts turned to how best she could get out of it.

"Fine. I'll go with you."

Sadko smiled. "Good. Now let's go."

"Where are we going?"

"Don't worry. You're not going to some rat-infested junk-hole. You actually get a stay at a ninth floor room overlooking the city for a couple of days. At least until we make the exchange."

"What exchange?"

"That's all I'm saying. Let's go." The two started walking down the hall before Mia suddenly stopped. "Move. Or I'll drop you right here."

"Wait. I can't go just yet."

"Why not?"

"I have to let them know I'm leaving."

"You're not even supposed to be here."

"How did you know that?"

Sadko continued with that evil grin of his. It was that smug type of look that a person gives when they know a big secret that no one else does, and they're proud of it. "Just a guess."

"No, it's seriously about a patient."

"You're stalling."

"I'm not. I just want to give the one doctor a message and then I'll go."

"I'm sure they'll figure things out."

"But if I don't tell them that the one baby needs a shot in the next ten minutes, the child will die. Please. The baby's in the NICU. All I want to do is give them the information to help the baby. And then I'll go."

"Fine."

"Can we go back up?"

Sadko shook his head. "No. Call whoever's up there and deliver the message."

"Can I have my phone?"

"Tell me who you want to call and I'll dial the number."

"Oh. Umm... her name is Sara."

Sadko took out Mia's phone and scrolled through the contacts. He finally found the one marked as Sara. "You say anything that doesn't sound like it involves a baby and I'll cut my losses right here and end you. Do you understand? I won't try again. I won't ask again. I will just put a bullet in your stomach right now and move on. You got it?"

Mia nodded. "I got it. No tricks."

Sadko dialed the number and gave the phone back to Mia. "I want it back when you're done."

Sara answered the phone. "Hey, Sara, it's me."

"What's up?"

"I forgot when I was up there to tell you about the Jones baby."

"The Jones baby? What?"

"You've got the east wing today, right?"

"Mia, you know I'm not working today, right?"

"OK, good. Now, the Jones baby needs that one shot we talked about within the next ten minutes or there will be some complications."

"Mia, are you all right?"

"Yeah, that's fine. Just tell Dr. Smith that I don't think the baby should be released until Sunday, though."

"I have no idea what you're talking about."

"C'mon, Sara, you know what I'm talking about. The Jones baby. It's an emergency."

"Oh my god. You're in trouble."

"Yes, that's the one." Sadko motioned with his finger that he wanted her to wrap it up. Mia nodded and put her hand up, asking for more time. "They just have to find the paperwork," she whispered to him.

She then put the phone back to her ear. "You got it, Sara?"

"Umm, yeah, I think so."

"OK, good. Now remember, I might have the next few days off, so the baby has to go up to the good room for this and he gets nine ml's of liquid, OK?"

"Oh my god, are you OK?"

"Just do what I'm telling you and everything should work out. You got it?"

"I got it."

"OK. Thank you."

"Please be careful."

Sadko motioned for her to wrap it up again. Mia took the phone away from her ear and handed it to him.

"Now let's go," Sadko said.

Mia complied and went with the man as they walked out of the hospital, just like they were any other couple.

"So what is the plan for me?" Mia asked.

"Beats me. Like I said, it's just a job. I'm just doing what I'm told."

"I assume I'm going to be used as bait."

Sadko looked at her and smiled again. "I think that's a good assumption."

19

By the time Recker got back to the office, Haley had already let Jones know what was happening with Mia. At least as how he understood it. Upon entering, Recker went over to the Keurig machine.

"I take it you secured Mia's protection before leaving?" Jones asked.

"Yeah. Malloy had some of his boys on the way there. Only had two or three guys available, but I guess it's better than nothing."

"I would imagine that she should still be adequately enough protected."

"That's the plan."

Recker put his drink down and joined the others at the desk, looking over some information they had on Jerrick. Recker wanted to try to pinpoint where he was as soon as possible. He'd only gotten a few minutes into his research when his phone rang. He looked at the phone curiously since it was an unknown number to him. He thought about not answering it and seeing if whoever it was would leave a message, but after four rings, decided to finally answer it.

"Hello?"

"Umm, hi."

"Hi. Who's this?"

"Oh, uh, my name's Sara. Are you Mike?"

"Uh, maybe. That would depend on who you are."

"Oh. I'm Sara."

"I know. You just said that. But who are you, how'd you get my number, and why are you calling me?"

"Oh, I'm sorry, I'm just nervous. I don't really know what's happening here. Mia just told me to call you if she was ever in trouble and gave me the code words and then I got a call from her and she said the words and then I had to find your number and..."

The woman was talking a little fast, and Recker was having a hard time figuring out what she was talking about. "Wait, wait, wait, just slow down. You're not making any sense."

"I'm sorry. Like I said, I'm just really nervous. And worried."

"It's OK. Just slow down and take a breath. Now what about Mia and how do you know her?"

"I work with Mia at the hospital."

"You're one of the nurses?"

"Yes. We're really close. I've worked at the hospital for about six years and she really helped me out so much when I first got hired. After that we became friends."

"And she told you she's in trouble?"

"Well, kind of, but not exactly."

"What?"

"OK, a long time ago, like, maybe two years ago, she told me that if she ever got into any trouble and she couldn't say exactly what it was, she would call me and give me a phrase to let me know she needed help. And she said that you were in some kind of secret government work, though she couldn't tell me exactly what you did."

"OK?"

"Anyway, she told me that if she ever called me with these code words, that I was to call you immediately and tell you about it. And she gave me this number, but she said to never call it under any circumstances unless it was under these conditions."

"OK. What was this phrase or words she said?"

"The words were Dr. Smith and the Jones baby."

As soon as Recker heard those names, he knew it really was from Mia and something was up. The hairs on the back of his neck stood up. Recker snapped his fingers to get both of his partner's attention.

"I need you to tell me exactly what she said."

"OK, well, she said something about the baby needing a shot. And that it was an emergency."

"What else? Did she say anything specifically?" Recker had hoped there was more to the message.

When they first got together, Recker had taught her how to give clues in messages without making it sound like she was saying anything at all. Just in the event something like this ever happened, and she was able to get a message to him, he would somehow be able to piece together the clues she left.

"Umm, she said something about the baby being released on Sunday."

"What else?"

"Uh, oh yeah, the only other thing she said was that the baby had to go up to the good room and that he needed nine ml's of liquid."

"That's what she said? Her exact words?"

"Yes."

"She said it had to go up to the good room?"

"Yes."

"And it needed nine ml's of liquid?"

"Those were her words."

"About how long ago was this?"

"Uh, maybe ten minutes tops. It took me a couple minutes to remember where I stashed the paper with your number on it."

"OK. Anything else?"

"No, that was it. But she sounded different. Not like worried or panicked or anything, but I could just tell her voice was different. Almost robotic-like."

"OK. Thank you for calling."

"Are you going to be able to figure out what she was talking about and help her? Because I'm so worried."

"I'll find her. Thanks."

Recker kept the phone pressed to his ear for the next few seconds, anger coursing through his veins. His fingers gripped the phone as hard as they could, as if he were trying to snap it like a twig. As his friends looked at him, they could see the rage building in his eyes and in his stance.

Jones finally broke the silence, getting the feeling that his friend wasn't going to say anything. "What about Mia?"

Recker's eyes finally softened and looked at his partner. "Huh?"

"In the conversation you just had, you mentioned Mia's name. It sounded as if there is some sort of trouble."

"Friend of hers. Said she got a weird phone call from her with a bunch of code words and stuff that made it seem like she was in trouble."

"What do you think?"

"I believe it."

"Why?"

"When I dropped her off, we agreed on her giving me a signal if she was in trouble. We agreed on the word Sunday. It was part of the message."

"Oh, my."

"But what about Vincent's guys?" Haley asked. "They're supposed to be there."

Recker looked at the time. "They're probably just

getting there about now. I can check with Malloy." He sighed. "I left her too soon."

"You can't blame yourself."

"I felt something was wrong. I just left her."

"It's not your fault."

Recker pulled up Malloy's number as he looked to Jones. "David, can you get into the hospital security footage?"

"I'm on it," Jones answered, immediately typing away. It wouldn't take long for him since it was a system he'd hacked his way into before and already knew how.

As Recker stepped away to call Malloy again, Haley moved closer to Jones, their shoulders almost touching.

"If Mia's gone..." Haley whispered.

Jones lifted his left hand off the keyboard to stop his friend from continuing his thought. "Let's not even go there."

Haley turned his head to look at Recker as he paced around the room. He then turned back to Jones. "If something happens to her, I can't imagine what he's gonna do."

It was Jones' turn to look at Recker now. He looked on at him sympathetically, his eyes beginning to tear up at the thought of more pain befalling his friend. He also whispered. "If something happens to Mia, hell will rain down. On everyone. No one will be safe. Including him."

Jones continued typing, and within a couple of minutes, both of their eyes lit up at what they were seeing on the screen.

"Oh jeez," Haley said. "Justin Sadko."

Jones zoomed in on the photo of Mia and Sadko leaving the hospital entrance. "There they are leaving together."

Jones leaned back and snapped his fingers to try to get Recker's attention. Recker immediately knew Jones had found something and quickly wrapped up his conversation with Malloy and rushed over to the desk.

"What'd you find?"

Jones pointed at the screen. "There it is. In full color."

"Sadko."

"Leading Mia out of the hospital as if nothing is wrong. No one is the wiser."

"I'm gonna kill him."

"Channel your energy and hatred into something positive at first," Jones said. "Don't let that hatred get in the way of thinking clearly. Let's find her first. Worry about everything else after that."

"I'm gonna kill him."

Jones put his hand on his friend's arm to help calm him down, though he knew that would be a difficult task. "Mike, I'm not trying to talk you down off the ledge or anything, but don't let thinking about the second step interfere with the first one. The first one, the most important one, is finding Mia before anything bad happens to her."

"Already has."

"I know, but if we can find her quickly, we can prevent a worse fate from falling upon her. Let's work to that end. You can get your revenge later. Let's just find her first."

Recker glared at his friend and partner before finally sighing and nodding. "OK."

"Let's think of the words she used carefully to see if there're any messages in there."

"There are. I taught her that if she was ever in trouble, to figure out how to slip in cues to an ordinary conversation so as other people wouldn't understand what she was saying."

"What about Malloy?" Haley asked. "What'd he say?"

"His guys just got there now."

"Didn't he have a guy in security? He might've seen what happened."

"Wasn't working today. I asked."

"Let's decipher Mia's message," Jones said.

"She said to take the baby up to the good room. That means wherever she was going, it's a nice place."

"That rules out the usual abandoned buildings and warehouses," Haley said.

"Up to the good room. That means there's more than one floor."

"A nice place that has more than one floor," Jones said, thinking of the possibilities.

"A hotel."

Jones nodded. "Possible. What other possibilities are there?"

"Maybe a nice office type building," Haley replied.

"Seems like a weird place to take her," Recker said. "A hotel would fit more."

"What else?" Jones asked.

"She said the number nine," Haley answered.

"Could be an address."

"Or a room number," Recker said.

"Or it could be a floor number," Haley said. "That would fit with going up to a room."

Recker nodded. "Could be. Could be any of those."

Jones swiveled his chair around and started typing again, drawing a look from his partners, who weren't sure if they had missed something.

"What are you doing?" Recker asked.

"Getting to work," Jones answered.

"But what are you working on?"

Jones stopped typing and looked at him. "The answer's not going to come to us. We have to go find it. So let's use the information we have up to this point and start digging."

"What information is that?"

"Our initial thoughts would indicate she may have been taken to a hotel, possibly the ninth floor. So let's get into all the local hotel's records and see if anyone recently checked into a ninth floor room in the last day or two. They most likely would not have had the room for much longer than that."

"You know how long that's gonna take?" Recker asked.

"I do." Jones then pointed to the other computers on the desk. "That's why it will go a lot faster if you two start helping."

Haley immediately sat down and started digging in. Recker, though, seemed a little more resistant.

"And what if we're wrong?" Recker asked. "What if they didn't take her there? What if they took her somewhere else, and we analyzed the clues wrong?"

"Then we'll move on to something else," Jones replied. "We can only start with what we have. We'll exhaust those possibilities first. If it's not there, then we'll move on to the next thing. That's what we do."

"You know how many hotels there are in this city? Let alone just outside of the city?"

"We can start off by ignoring those without nine floors. That will make it go a little faster."

"Maybe it doesn't have anything to do with a ninth floor."

"Maybe it doesn't. But like I said, it's a start. So let's start with it."

Recker took a deep breath, then sat down on one of the chairs. "There are thousands of hotel rooms in this city."

"I'm putting into the database to only spit out

hotels with at least nine floors," Jones said. "That should only take a minute or two. Once we get that, we can filter it to people who've checked in within the past three days. I doubt Sadko would have checked in before that. If we filter it further to checking the ninth floors first, it won't be as daunting as it initially appears."

"Assuming he even used his real name."

"Even if he didn't, once we start investigating, we'll find that out pretty quick."

"We can also check out cameras in the lobbies," Haley said. "Some of the bigger ones have them."

"Yeah, once we have it narrowed down to some possibilities then I can dig into security footage too."

Within a couple of minutes, hundreds of hotels in the Greater Philadelphia area popped up as having ninth floors. Recker sighed, knowing this was going to take a while. It was time that Mia might not have had. Nonetheless, as Jones rightly pointed out, it was the best and only lead they really had at the moment. They just had to plow through it as quickly as possible.

An hour went by and they didn't seem to be any closer to finding Mia. They were able to check off several hotels that didn't have anyone check in on a ninth floor within the previous few days, but there were plenty more that did, and the background had to be checked on all of them.

"Wait a minute," Jones said.

"You got something?" Recker asked.

"No, I just have an idea. I don't know why I didn't think of this before."

"What?"

"A picture of Mia. I have one in the computer here."

"So?"

"So I can put her picture through the facial recognition software and match it up against all the security footage that I can pull out from the different hotel chains."

"Do it," Recker hurriedly said.

"What if they took her to one of the ones that don't have the cameras?" Haley said.

"Then we'll go back to Plan A," Jones replied. "I don't know why I didn't think of this initially. I completely forgot that I had her picture in here to match it up."

"Why do you?" Recker asked.

"I have pictures of all of us in here. You, me, Chris, Mia, Tyrell, even Vincent and Malloy."

"Why?"

"For precisely this very reason. In the event any one of us ever went missing, we could run the picture through the facial rec software so we can locate the one of us that's missing."

Recker looked at Jones' screen, desperately hoping that a match would soon appear. "How long's this gonna take?"

"Shouldn't take long."

"Long to you or long to me?"

"The longer process is getting into the hotel's security footage. From there it's easy. Running her picture through only takes a few minutes. It's getting the footage that takes longer."

Recker couldn't just sit there and watch the process unfold in front of him. He got up and started pacing around the room. In most cases his pacing bothered Jones, but in this instance, it didn't bother him at all. He figured the pacing would help to calm Recker down. Even if it was just a little. As Recker paced and waited, his phone rang. It was Malloy again.

"Just wanted to see how you were making out?"

"Still looking," Recker replied. "It was Sadko, though."

"Sadko? You sure?"

"Positive. Got a picture from the hospital of them leaving together."

Malloy seethed into the phone. "Bastard. Haven't found anything else?"

"Checking hotel camera footage."

"Hotels? You think he took her there?"

"She left me a coded message. That's kind of what we're assuming. Not a hundred percent sure on it, but that's what we're going with right now."

"OK, well, I'm not gonna keep you. I'll let you get back to it. But if you need us, I got a few guys, plus me, waiting on standby. If you find her and need backup, just give me the word and we'll be there in a second."

"I appreciate that."

Haley saw Recker put the phone back in his pocket. "Who was that?"

"Malloy. Wanted to see how it was going. Also said if we need him then he'll be there. Just have to give him the word."

"That's good. We might."

"Assuming we find her," Recker said.

Jones felt it was his responsibility to keep his friend's spirits up. He wasn't going to let Recker get too down or give up hope. "We'll find her. We'll find her."

20

Jones stopped the feed from continuing, seeing exactly what he hoped to see. What he needed to see. There it was on the screen. A picture of Mia and Sadko going through the front hotel entrance. Jones leaned back in his chair, satisfied with his efforts so far.

"I've got them."

Recker rushed over to him while Haley just pushed his chair over.

"That's them," Recker said. "Where are they?"

"This picture was from The Lingford Hotel. Taken approximately two hours ago."

"She's there. Let's go."

"Wait," Jones said. "Just wait."

"For what?"

"Let's have a plan first before you go charging in half-cocked."

"Ain't no half-cocked about it. I'm going in full blast."

"I know. Let me pull up information on the hotel so we know what room you're charging into."

"It's about twenty-five minutes to get there. Tell me on the way. Mia's not waiting extra time."

Recker rushed over to the gun cabinet and removed a couple of weapons. Haley did the same. After quickly getting themselves ready, they ran toward the door.

"Call me when you have something," Recker said as the two of them exited the office.

Jones continued working for the next few minutes, not taking long to find out what they needed. He immediately called Recker to let him know.

"What's up?" Recker asked.

"The room they are staying in is number nine-one-two."

"You sure?"

"Pretty sure. The room is registered to a Randall Moore."

"Moore. Isn't that the same name that Jerrick used the other day when I met with him?"

"It is. And they used the same address associated with that name."

As they drove to the hotel, Recker and Haley tried to come up with a plan. Well, it was mostly Haley trying to come up with one. Recker only had one plan in mind. Charge in, find Mia, and kill whoever got in their way.

"Should we try like we did it last time?" Haley asked. "Me finding a nearby building and covering you from there?"

"Don't think we have that kind of time to wait."

"Yeah, plus it's the middle of the day so every building's going to be occupied."

"And I think it'll be better if we go in together. Who knows what we'll run into when we go in, so I think it'll be better if we're side by side."

Haley double checked his gun. "Sounds good."

"Sure you wanna do this? We know this is a trap to lure me in. Who knows what we'll be walking into?"

"Is that even a question? You and Mia are like family. If we go down, we go down together."

Recker nodded, then pushed his foot further down on the gas pedal. They arrived at the hotel in just over twenty minutes. They stood just outside the hotel. They put their earpieces in and Recker called Jones.

"David, we're here."

"I'll try to support you however I can from here."

"We might need help getting in that room."

"I've already checked and this hotel only has the electronic keycards for entering rooms, so they don't even have knobs with keyholes in them."

"Can you get us in?"

"I should be able to remotely unlock it, but you'll

have to let me know when you're there so I don't unlock it too early."

"OK. We'll let you know."

Recker looked to his partner. "Be on the lookout to see if they have any guards in the lobby."

"Right."

They calmly walked into the hotel. Calm on the outside. On the inside, Recker was a burning and simmering rage of anger that was about to blow. They took a quick look around the lobby, but didn't see anyone that matched up with being one of Jerrick's men. Recker memorized a few of their faces from the last encounter he had with them. With no trouble looming from the lobby, and nobody to alert Sadko on the ninth floor of their presence, the two of them went to the stairs. Recker stopped, thinking better of them going up together.

"Maybe we should split up. Just in case they're waiting."

Haley agreed. "I'll take the elevator. We'll get there from different angles."

"I'll let you know when I get in position."

Recker started ascending the steps as Haley hurried over to the elevator. He had to wait about thirty seconds for the doors to open. He was the only one to get on.

"Chris, can you hear me?" Jones asked.

"I hear you."

"I switched over to a private line so Mike can't hear."

"Why?"

"You'll need to be the voice of reason when you get into that room."

"What do you mean?"

"You have to be prepared for the possibility that... that you may not find Mia in the way that you're used to."

"What are you saying?"

"In the event that they have... I don't even want to say the words. But in the event that they've decided she's outlived her usefulness..."

"Don't even think it."

"I don't want to think it. But we have to understand the realities of who we are dealing with. And if that ungodly horror becomes reality, and he sees that, then you are going to have to walk him off the ledge."

"Do you know something that you're not telling?"

"No. And I hope to god that I'm wrong for even thinking it. But it is something we have to consider the possibilities of. And if the unthinkable becomes true, he is going to need help."

"If that scenario becomes true, I don't think it's him that's gonna need the help. And I don't think I could stop him."

"I'm praying that we won't have to."

Haley watched the number above the doors hit the red nine. "This is my stop. Gotta go."

Recker was just hitting the floor at the same time. It was a big hotel, so it wasn't a straight hallway, and the floors wrapped around. He went down the first hallway, then turned to his left, passing a bunch of rooms. He came to the edge of the next hallway, then peeked down and saw Haley walking his way. Recker became more relaxed as he saw his friend coming closer.

"This place is bigger than I thought," Recker said.

"Which way?"

Recker pointed behind him. "Well I just came from back there. I think the room's that way." He pointed to their right.

They walked down the hallway, eventually finding the door they were looking for at the far end of it, on the right-hand side.

"Surprised there are no guards," Haley said.

"Guess they don't want to advertise something's going on in there."

"Yeah."

"David, we're at the door."

"Give me a moment," Jones replied. "Should have it within a few seconds."

Recker and Haley both put their hands on their weapons, not yet withdrawing them in case someone happened to walk by. They each took a deep breath.

"You know, I just thought, if this goes on for more than a few minutes, police are going to be called," Haley said.

"No doubt."

"If we can't escape quickly, we might not be able to get out."

"I know. Still wanna do this?"

Haley nodded. "Let's do it."

They then heard the clicking sound of the door being unlocked. Recker put his hand on the door and turned the handle, quickly opening it and thrusting it open as the two of them jumped inside the room. Recker threw himself to the floor, pointing his gun and ready to fire at the first target, while Haley ducked to the right, dropping to one knee, ready to do the same. But there was no one in the room. There was no one to fight. And no one to fight back.

Recker motioned to his partner to start checking out the other rooms, while he took the kitchen. Haley went into the first bedroom, emerging only a minute later. After Recker cleared the kitchen area, he then took the second bedroom, while Haley took the bathroom. They met back up in the short hallway separating the rooms.

"They're not here," Recker said with a sigh.

"David, room's empty," Haley said. "Completely empty."

"I've looked at the footage and I did not see her leave the hotel. I'll check again."

As they waited on further word from Jones, Recker and Haley double checked the room to see if they could find any clues as to where they'd gone. A few minutes later, Jones got back on the line.

"She's gone."

"What do you mean she's gone?" Recker asked.

"There's a side door. They took her out through there."

"When?"

"Roughly forty-five minutes ago. Sadko and two other men."

Recker sighed. "We'll never find her now."

"There's a camera on the outside of the building, not the inside. So I got a good look at the vehicle, including the plates. I'm running it through the other cameras located throughout the city. If another camera picks it up, I can see if I can figure out where they're heading."

Haley tapped Recker on the arm. "Let's keep looking and see if we can find something."

"There's nothing here."

"Let's check again."

Recker took the living room, while Haley checked the bedroom. Once they were finished, Recker took the second bedroom, while Haley checked the bathroom. He initially overlooked it, but upon a second glance, he saw it. A small piece of a necklace was hanging out of the corner of the cabinet underneath the sink. Haley got down on one knee and pulled the necklace out to look at it. It was the one that Recker had just given to Mia.

"Mike!"

Recker immediately came running in. "What?"

Haley held the necklace up. "It's hers."

"Where'd you find it?"

"Hanging out of this cabinet." Haley then opened the cabinet. He looked inside and then saw a wad of toilet paper off to the side.

"What's that?"

"I don't know. Weird spot to have a bunch of toilet paper sitting, though."

He started to unravel it out of curiosity, then saw something that piqued his interest. Somewhere in the middle of it, it looked like some words written. They were a little faded and hard to read, but he could make it out.

"You got something?" Recker asked.

"Looks like an address."

"Let me see." Haley handed the toilet paper to Recker. "This is Mia's handwriting."

"She left us a clue."

A small smile came over Recker's face. He still had hope. "She left the necklace hoping we'd figure out she was here, then find the necklace, then see this."

"You taught her well."

"David, I think we know where she's going." Recker gave him the address. It was an area he was familiar with, though he didn't know the exact address.

"It's in the Upper Darby area."

"Jeremiah's old stomping grounds."

"A quick search turns up a single-family house. Could be vacant. Not sure."

"We're on the way."

Recker and Haley flew out of the room and scurried down the steps to get out of the hotel as quickly as possible. They jumped into their car and started toward the address that Mia left them.

"Let's bring backup," Recker said.

"Malloy?"

"They're after Sadko too. No reason we should have to do this alone."

Haley nodded. "I agree. The more the merrier."

Recker immediately called Malloy. "Hey, I think we know where Sadko is. You want in?"

Malloy snickered. "Are you kidding? Just name the place."

"Upper Darby. We're on our way there now. They've got Mia so I don't know how long I can wait for you."

"I can be there in twenty."

"That's probably when we'll get there. I'll text you the address."

"I'm leaving now."

By the time Recker and Haley got to the address, they saw several cars out in front of the house. They confirmed with Jones that the one car was the one that was used to take Mia.

"I've been here before," Recker said.

"You have?"

"A long time ago. I met Jeremiah here once. I knew

that address sounded familiar. I just couldn't place it. But I remember it now."

"What's the inside look like?"

"Back then it was bare. A couple tables and chairs, not much more. Never saw the upstairs. Just the main floor. Jeremiah only used it as a meeting place."

"Looks like the disciple's picked up old habits."

"Yeah."

"How long we gonna wait for Malloy?"

"I think we can wait a few minutes. With Mia in there, I'm not waiting much longer than that."

"What if they moved her again somewhere else? Or maybe this wasn't where they were taking her. Maybe she overheard just an address."

Recker took a deep breath. "I'm trying to think positively. She's in there."

Not even a minute later, Recker noticed a few figures moving out of the corner of his eye. He turned his head and saw the familiar face of Malloy coming closer. He was crouching down as he moved to avoid being spotted by anyone in the house, though they were all further down the street anyway and unlikely to be seen from it.

"How's it looking?" Malloy asked.

"No movement yet," Recker answered.

"Sure they're in there?"

"Not sure of anything yet."

"Well let's hope that they are."

"That's about all I'm running on at the moment."

"I got ten men with me. I got six on the back. They'll go in when we give the word."

"That should work."

"Any idea how many they got in there?"

Recker shook his head. "Nope."

"Don't matter. We'll give them hell no matter how many they got."

"How you wanna play this?" Haley asked. "Without knowing where Mia is, if we go charging in and shooting wildly, she might get caught in the crossfire. Or they might just target her first."

"But if we wait too long, something equally horrible might happen," Malloy said.

"It's a gamble either way," Recker said. He thought for a few seconds to figure out how he wanted to play it. The only thing that mattered to him at that moment was just getting Mia out. He didn't care about revenge. He didn't care about getting even. Sadko didn't even enter his mind. It was only about what was best for Mia. "The longer she's in there, the worse off she'll be. We go in and take her."

"How?" Haley asked.

Recker looked to Malloy. "Can you have your men in the back break in first?"

Malloy nodded, knowing what he was thinking. "They'll scurry to the back thinking the action's back there and then we'll come through the front."

"We'll give them a few seconds of a head start so if they don't see anyone out here, they'll think everyone's coming through the back and bring everyone back there."

"Lighten our load."

"You good with that?"

"Let's do it." Malloy immediately contacted his men in back of the house and instructed them to go forward. "Let's see what shakes out."

Within a few seconds, they started to hear gunfire. They resisted the urge to join for a good solid minute.

"Let's go!" Recker said.

The three of them, along with the other four men that Malloy brought along, all raced to the front of the house, cutting through the lawns of the neighbor's property.

"Two of you stay and cover through the front window," Malloy told his men.

With the gunfire still plainly heard, the others broke toward the front door, charging at it with all their might, breaking right through it. Almost immediately they were under a barrage of gunfire. Several men showed up from other rooms and started shooting at them, with Recker and the team firing back. It seemed like it took forever to dispatch the men, but in reality it was under a minute. With everyone out of their way, Recker led the team through the house as the gunfire suddenly fell silent.

"We're good back here," one of Malloy's men said.

"Good here too," Malloy replied.

"Maybe that's it," Haley said.

"But where's Mia?" Recker asked.

Malloy directed several of his men to check the upstairs while they continued downstairs. They went through a couple of rooms downstairs before finally coming to what used to be a bedroom. The door was closed. Recker took a step back, then kicked at the knob, the door flying wide open. With Haley and Malloy behind him, Recker stepped foot into the bedroom. His eyes were immediately drawn to Mia, sitting in a wooden chair in the middle of the room. Her hands and feet were tied, her mouth had a handkerchief stuffed in it, but he didn't notice any cuts or bruises on her. Standing behind her was Justin Sadko. He had a gun pointed at the back of her head.

"Let me out of here or I'll blow a hole through her head."

"You're not leaving unless you let her go," Recker said.

"Oh no. She's my insurance policy."

"OK. You've used it. Let her go and I give you my word I won't kill you." Recker tossed his gun on the ground. "All I want is her. You can go."

Recker noticed Sadko's finger was on the trigger of his gun. One wrong move, one twitch from him and Mia's life was over. They could've easily shot him now if they wanted to. But Recker couldn't take the chance of his finger pulling the trigger on his way down, ending Mia's life.

"I put my gun down. All I want is her. You can go."

Sadko shook his head. "I don't trust you. I let her go and I'm done."

"You're not leaving her with her. You're not. So the only option you have is to trust me. You can either let her go and live. Or you can stay here and you can die. Those are your two options. I'm not letting you leave here with her."

Sadko looked at Haley and Malloy, both of whom still had their guns pointed at him. "I let her go, I know I'm dead."

Recker looked at his friends. "Put your guns down."

They both looked at him, and though neither particularly liked the request, they both did as they were asked. They both lowered their weapons, though neither got rid of them.

"Untie her," Recker said. "Let her go. Once she's with me, then I'm done with you and you can go. It's your only option."

"Or I could just blow her head off first."

Haley and Malloy both instantly raised their weapons again, ready to fire. Recker stuck his hand out to stop them.

"If you do that, you're dead," Recker said. "If you want to live, your only chance is giving her back to me. That's it." He motioned to his partners to lower their weapons again. They complied.

Sadko licked his lips as he considered his options. After a minute, he finally decided to take the chance. He took out his pocket knife and cut the straps holding

Mia's legs and wrists together. He gave her a slight push on her back to get her moving. Mia ran over to Recker and hugged him tight.

"As soon as she's gone you can go," Recker said.

Recker looked at Haley, who nodded at him to take Mia out. Recker put his arm around her and escorted her out of the room. They gave them a few seconds for Recker to get Mia out of the house. Haley and Malloy continued to stand there, staring down Sadko. Malloy looked at him with such contempt. A former colleague who sold them out.

"You lousy traitor," Malloy said.

"Nothing personal, Jimmy," Sadko said. "I just found a better offer."

"You no good low-life."

"Well, it's been real. But I think I'll go now."

"You're not going anywhere."

"You heard what he said. A deal's a deal. He gave me his word."

Almost in unison, Haley and Malloy raised their weapons and opened fire, killing Sadko immediately. Once Mia heard the sound of the shots outside, she flinched. Recker looked at her and smiled.

"It's over," Recker said.

"What took you so long?" Mia joked.

"I must be slowing down in my old age."

After it was over, Haley and Malloy walked over to Sadko's body and stood over it.

"I didn't give you my word," Haley said.

"Me neither," Malloy said, spitting on the body. "Trash."

"Let's get out of here before the cops come."

Once they were outside, they stood there for a few moments before going their separate ways.

"Gotta admit," Malloy said. "Didn't think you had that in you."

"Mia's like a sister to me. I wasn't letting him get away with that. Or maybe you're just rubbing off on me."

Malloy laughed. "Maybe there's hope for you yet."

Once Malloy and his men walked off, Haley met back up with Recker and Mia, giving her a hug.

"Thanks for coming for me," Mia said.

"I'm just glad you're OK," Haley replied.

"He's dead, isn't he?"

"It's over. There's nothing else to worry about."

"This time. What about the next time? I'm sure there'll be one."

"Next time we'll be ready."

"For some of us, there's always a next time," Recker said. "But for you, this is over. For the rest of us, we'll worry about the next time when it gets here. And we will be ready."

ABOUT THE AUTHOR

Mike Ryan is a USA Today Bestselling Author. He lives in Pennsylvania with his wife, and four children. He's the author of the bestselling Silencer Series, as well as many others. Visit his website at www.mikeryanbook s.com to find out more about his books, and sign up for his newsletter. You can also interact with Mike via Facebook, and Instagram.

ALSO BY MIKE RYAN

Keep reading with the next book in The Silencer Series - Recoil.

The Extractor Series

The Eliminator Series

The Cain Series

The Ghost Series

The Brandon Hall Series

The Last Job

A Dangerous Man

The Crew

Printed in Great Britain
by Amazon

23726528R00139